BIRTH CANAL

Dias Novita Wuri (1989) was born in Jakarta, Indonesia. She graduated from Universitas Indonesia, majoring in Russian Language and Literature. In 2019, she earned a master's degree in Comparative Literature from Queen Mary University of London. She has had short stories published in Indonesian newspapers since 2012. Her first book, *Makramé*, was published in 2017 by Gramedia Pustaka Utama, and was on the Khatulistiwa Literary Award longlist in 2018. Her second book, *Jalan Lahir*, was published in 2021 by Kepustakaan Populer Gramedia. She served as adviser in the literary section of the editorial board of jakartabeat.net.

DIAS NOVITA WURI

BIRTH CANAL

SCRIBE
Melbourne • London

For Renke

Scribe Publications
2 John Street, Clerkenwell, London WC1N 2ES, United Kingdom
18–20 Edward St, Brunswick, Victoria 3056, Australia
3754 Pleasant Ave, Suite 100, Minneapolis, Minnesota 55409, USA

First published in Indonesian as *Jalan Lahir* by
Kepustakaan Populer Gramedia in 2021
Published in English by Scribe 2023

Typeset in Portrait by the publishers

Printed and bound in the UK by CPI Group (UK) Ltd, Croydon CR0 4YY

Scribe Publications is committed to the sustainable use of natural resources
and the use of paper products made responsibly from those resources.

978 1 914484 68 1 (UK edition)
978 1 957363 62 2 (US edition)
978 1 922585 76 9 (Australian edition)
978 1 761385 29 2 (ebook)

Catalogue records for this book are available from the
National Library of Australia and the British Library.

scribepublications.co.uk
scribepublications.com
scribepublications.com.au

PART ONE

You are on a mission
to rescue your beloved.
She left on an earlier wave
and your plan was to wait for her

NORMAN ERIKSON PASARIBU
SEEKING ANOTHER EARTH (YOUR PRE-AESCHYLEAN
PLAY IN THREE ACTS)
(TRANSLATED BY TIFFANY TSAO)

NASTITI

One of the men was a photographer. 'You are incredibly beautiful,' he liked to say to her, and the first time he did so was as they inadvertently passed each other, on the sidewalk of Jalan Jenderal Sudirman, who knows how many months ago. It was a few minutes after dusk, and the roads were congested in all directions. Cars had started turning on their low-beam headlights, which then half-heartedly illuminated various flat surfaces. The usual city landscape. The sky had a rosy nuance that somehow seemed both warm and sad, like a freshly slapped cheek. In the midst of all that, the man was wandering around, aiming at mysterious objects with a large digital camera that hung around his neck, and then he saw Nastiti. 'You are incredibly beautiful,' he declared matter-of-factly. Nastiti only smiled in return (she was confused, but nobody would have guessed it). 'Stand there,' said the man. 'The light is right. You shine like an angel.'

So Nastiti did just that. It didn't occur to her not to. Later, she would think that the scene might have seemed rather outlandish to the dozens of people around her, all moving along the same pavement at varying degrees of speed. But then there she was, Nastiti, standing between a bush and a street vendor selling greasy golden fritters, looking straight ahead, without any particular expression, as the man snapped her picture. Indeed, that is the man's job: his function in this life is to capture the beauty of such ordinary, everyday poses. In fact, Nastiti herself was something everyday in nature, just ordinary; a girl who was going home from some boring office job. 'You always carry all those bags?' the man asked. 'What's in there — shoes?' Nastiti shrugged and pointed to the ugly rubber flip-flops she was wearing. 'These are for walking on the sidewalks and in the bus,' she explained. 'The ones in the bag are for the office.' That was the beginning.

Recently, we could actually see this very photograph in a collective exhibition of street photographers at a trendy art gallery in South Jakarta; Nastiti's figure adorned a piece of white wall in the middle of forty other photographs — tired, dishevelled faces, a thousand sorts of city people that told us stories of chaotic and crazy metropolitan life through their still images. Some, like Nastiti, were young and beautiful women, wearing pencil skirts and office-style blouses and cardigans, the artificial colour on their lips already half-faded. The same photograph also appeared in one of the prestigious national newspapers in an article reviewing the exhibition. We saw Nastiti in the corner on page ten, we counted three tiny pimples scattered on her forehead. She emitted a golden aura even though the photo in the paper was printed in black-and-white. (*You shine like an angel.*)

She said the term 'street photographer' was somewhat unfair. According to Nastiti, these people were glamorous. 'You know, he's had exhibitions everywhere. You know, Hong Kong, Singapore, everywhere.' In her mind she was picturing tall glass buildings gleaming under the sun, a large green open garden, and in the midst of it all were the man's works. Sometimes Nastiti's innocence could seem as bare as peeled fruit, but that was only because she was allowing it. Other times she could close herself off completely. For now, she was fascinated by the fact that the man's camera was a Pentax 645Z, and that it cost about the same as a car. And that the man was the brightest young rising star in the street photography scene in Southeast Asia, something that intrigued her more than she was willing to admit. Nastiti was fascinated with her own face against the white wall. 'I mean,' she said at the time, 'that girl is me. But she doesn't seem like me either.' We went to the exhibition together once, and once I went alone, without her. I stood in front of her photograph for a full twenty minutes, staring at it. At that moment I thought with certainty that I knew her. Now I'm not sure.

When she disappeared, I looked for her in the apartment she shared with her mother. The older woman welcomed me into her living room, and she seemed oblivious and relaxed. 'Oh, if I remember correctly, Titi went out of town for company business, eh. She left a message on the fridge door. I think she'll only return next week, eh.' Frustration coursed through my body like electricity, but I couldn't say any more, and the many 'eh's uttered by Nastiti's mother really hurt my head. Besides, I suddenly also saw the photo on the coffee table; it was another Nastiti, this time in black-and-white, outlined by a white wooden rectangle (white to match everything else in that compact, minimalist apartment), the man's work that no one had ever exhibited or reviewed because it was made privately for Nastiti. The photo was a close-up: she dominated the entire frame, even though her hands were covering her face. In the photo she protested and turned away, but she displayed it where anyone could see it.

Here I would like to quote Dejan Stojanović, the Serbian poet: *My feelings are too loud for words and too shy for the world.* Hardly anyone noticed when Nastiti disappeared from the surface of the earth.

―――――――

7

She had told me that she was going to 'a place'. That was all. Deep inside, she knew she'd care if someone (for example, me) tried to find her, but at the same time she didn't care. She travelled. She walked until she was exhausted, despite the way she'd trained her leg muscles by running on the treadmill and attending bone-crushing aerobics classes, which she faithfully participated in twice a week. She carried only a small drawstring bag containing a dead mobile phone, a few things she didn't want to think about, and her wallet, and her mind spiralled around that ridiculous wallet: the credit and debit cards in it, the multifunctional e-money card, the access card for her office, some crumpled notes. She had a habit of spending too much time keeping the contents of her wallet in order, all the time, imagining how easily it could be snatched away by a dirty pickpocket, any time, and then she would be stranded on the street, helpless. *Maybe that would have been better*, she thought, *being stranded*; then she walked on. At no point was she thinking about me; she had no idea that thirty kilometres away I was riding around on my motorbike, worrying about her and wanting to cry.

So then Nastiti entered a nearby 7-Eleven to withdraw some more notes from an ATM. It's possible it was already half past eight in the evening, but she couldn't be completely sure; she wasn't the kind of person to wear a wristwatch and her mobile had been off for hours. The convenience store felt like a movie set — there was just never a 7-Eleven as empty as that one was, so something must have been wrong somewhere: there must have been a secret plot, as if someone had deliberately removed the horde of snot-nosed junior high school kids who normally performed all their social interactions at 7-Elevens. Nastiti bought a steaming-hot drink in a tall paper cup, sprinkled it with cinnamon powder, then sat on a frail metal bench in front of the store's parking lot to sip the drink. Her mind was full, all over the place; she thought, *a city is a stretch of velvet covered with rubies*, perhaps like the fabric that Nadia Lukito, her long-forgotten childhood friend, turned into haute couture dresses at school at Esmod. The rubies were fake, but the sparkle was stunning, nonetheless. Where was Nadia now? What had she, Nastiti, done that their friendship came to an end? She remembered reading Nadia's name in a magazine a while ago (Nadia was now a decent fashion designer) and felt her throat tighten. She remembered endless days of sitting in her office, staring at that stretch of velvet studded with rubies from the height of the eleventh floor, wondering where she really was.

She didn't charge her phone. She'd do it at some point, but right now she wasn't going to do anything with it. At last, she took a deep breath and got up from the bench. She knew where she was headed and knew that it was time to go. She knew what 'a place' meant, her singular destination.

There they were: her palms, facing up towards you. 'Maybe if we take a good look at all these lines,' she said, her eyes gleaming, 'we'd be able to tell that my poor dad would be run over by a semi-trailer on the freeway.' She smiled ironically. 'I mean, you know, before anything happened. I'd want someone to warn me.' Upon hearing that, I cupped her hands with my own. You'd notice that her fingers resembled twigs; each nail was painted a plain colour — perhaps milky cream or a pale pinkish hue, whatever — but what was clear to me was that the shape of her nails was captivating, small and not elegant, but still perfect. Next, you'd notice the texture of her skin. Nastiti liked washing dishes, for some reason, and her skin felt like craft paper. Maybe crepe.

I made no comment. Nastiti continued, 'I'm somebody who believes in stupid things. On that day, there were all kinds of bad omens floating in the air.'

'Such as?'

'Hmm. My glass fell on the floor during breakfast and shattered? The classic.'

I snorted. 'Sure.'

'I believe in palm-reading. Some have said that my lines are brimming with bad luck.'

'Bullshit,' I said.

'Did you know that some people surgically create new lines on their palms to change bad luck? Sounds like it's worth trying.'

She had told those men, her lovers — not all, just some of them — this special story; only God knew how Nastiti decided which ones were worthy enough to hear it and which weren't. I knew it because I had known her for a long time. I was on the scene almost as soon as she called me. I saw everything. You know, there are times when someone won't be able to cry even though they want to. That's what I remember most clearly about Nastiti at that moment, as she slumped in my arms, vomiting up sour-smelling liquid onto the thighs of my jeans. She was shaking violently, in complete distress but unable to cry.

'Got cigs?' asked Nastiti out of nowhere. She didn't smoke.

'Always.'

She expertly took a cigarette from my pack of Marlboro menthols, then lit it with my cheap gas lighter. This was the first time I had seen her smoke, while I usually smoked a pack a day, or two packs if my life was really going berserk. But her movements were almost identical to mine, as if she had smoked all her life. Smoke billowed out of her nostrils after a short journey through her trachea and her red, throbbing wet lungs; the smoke danced, the tip of her cigarette twinkled in the almost-darkness. We were out in the open, on the roof of my boarding house, awkwardly sitting on a square cement block that numbed our buttocks in less than ten minutes; the drying laundry around us, blown by the wind. Nastiti finished her cigarette and reached for another. (Only later did I find out that she always smoked when she was with one of the guys, one who was a smoker like me.)

'Wow. Aren't you loving that,' I said, dumbfounded.

'It's delicious,' she said.

'Huh. I don't think you know what that means.'

The expression on her face didn't change. She grabbed my hand in the same way she had the cigarette pack. 'Have a look. There are three lines: the head line, the life line, and the heart line. Each line describes your character. For example, look here. *Your* head line is long and straight, which means you think too much.' Her index finger tickled.

'Oh.'

'I know the basics. But I don't know how to read bad luck.' Nastiti put her cigarette out on the cement block then stared at her palms. I was afraid of what might be on her mind every time she became silent and unreadable. 'Nas,' I said. 'Oi, Nas.'

'What?'

'Eh. Never mind.'

She frowned. I muttered, 'I mean — the accident was a long time ago.'

Slowly she nodded. 'My lines are very thin. Maybe that's the source of the bad luck?' she asked. 'Maybe thin lines mean one would accidentally cause her father's death.'

'But my lines are also thin. Here.' I showed her. I winced at the sight of my thick fleshy palms with calluses here and there, the result of riding a motorbike in Jakarta's traffic jams every day. 'And you didn't cause his death,' I added, softer.

'Maybe it was my mother's doing,' said Nastiti.

'Nas, stop it.'

She obediently closed her mouth, as if I had cast a spell. Even so, I knew that she was still engulfed in the memory. Only five years earlier, when she had just started high school, she had witnessed a freak car accident that had taken the life of her father, a quiet man who opened his mouth only occasionally — and only to express displeasure. So, quite the tragedy. I never knew in detail what had happened between Nastiti and her father that day, except that they'd had a huge argument in the car, in the middle of the freeway, on their way to pick up Nastiti's mother from the airport (she was working as a senior flight attendant for one of the national airlines). Her father had pulled over to the side of the road, ordered Nastiti to get out of the car, and left her there. However, she still got to witness how, not too much further along, her father suddenly lost control of the car and collided with a semi-trailer. She told me, a year later, 'Perhaps it was because of something that I had said. Or my mother. At that moment they were also arguing on the phone.' Everything was so vague, and she had never told me more. I was the person on whom Nastiti liked to dump any toxic waste that burdened her mind, but I never had the power to determine how much she would give me.

'But how can ...' I'd said, helplessly. Nastiti had shrugged — a gesture that was steadily becoming her trademark.

It had happened on a Saturday morning, when the freeway was relatively empty, except for a bunch of speeding taxis whose drivers undoubtedly were made euphoric by these kilometres of freedom in front of them. I arrived in broad daylight like a hero who came too late; not helpful and not needed. In my dreams, later, the daylight always became twilight, with an unnatural dark-blue sky hanging very close above my head, but the sequence of events remained the same: Nastiti kneeling in a strange position on the asphalt was the same, the sound of an ambulance and/or a police car siren wailing, stuffy air pressing our chests with a pair of invisible giant hands, other cars creeping through it all, and in the distance, we saw what remained of the black Honda Civic owned by Nastiti's father and the semi-trailer that it collided with — all the same. Nastiti's voice squeaked so faintly amidst the temporary madness that overtook her. *Papa died?* My own father had died of diabetes earlier that year; I had been there when he departed from this world and out of his blind, groping, emaciated body. This time I saw Nastiti's father on the side of the freeway, covered by several sheets of yesterday afternoon's newspaper. We took one breath, and Nastiti and I became these lost children without fathers. It felt so horrible, so lonely.

I went with her in the ambulance — her swollen, sour lips pressed against my shoulder. I felt the warmth of her breath on my arm, almost sticky, strange. You know what, maybe that warm thing was actually her consciousness, slowly rising from the depths of her soul while she leaned against me. Along the way she passed out and I let her, because wasn't it better like that?

'Whoops, there's only one cig left,' said the Nastiti on the roof, her laughter flying with the wind.

Did I love her? Yes. Did she love me?

I cared enough to pose the same question to some of those men. 'Do you even love her? Huh?' I was like a hungry creature, emerging from the depths of a marsh, my stiff hands reaching forward, ready to choke the men's necks. But that's all bullshit, of course, because I never did it (choking, I mean) even though my hands were dying to. Hell, it felt like I was even ready to kill. I just didn't: instead, I faced them as fellow men and not beasts, and we had more or less civilised conversations, in which I sat swallowing everything I would have shouted in their faces had I not exercised extraordinary self-control. Do they love her? *Yes. I don't know. No.*

There they were, sitting opposite me in some cafe-of-the-moment, tiny espresso cups on the table, or beside me in the first street seafood tent that came into sight. I studied their faces and replayed Nastiti's words about them in my head while they blurted, 'Oh, you're *that* friend of hers.' (What kind of friend, Nas?) In fact, none of these men knew each other, nor were they connected to each other in any way, let alone to me. I knew their names only because Nastiti had dragged them into my life through a series of stories that seemed endless: different men appeared and disappeared, one day they'd be there and the next, gone for good. One of them asked me how Nastiti was doing. Others stared right through me, fixing their gazes on the ornate pot of mini cacti or the fans that were noisily whirring on the ceiling. One of them asked, 'How much do you know about us? I don't want my wife to find out.' In the end, my miserable adventure culminated in Bintaro, in a sector known for its fancy houses. I found my destination in an instant — the man's house was the biggest and tackiest — and without taking off my helmet or jacket, I picked up a rock the size of a tennis ball that happened to be lying in a vacant lot nearby, and I threw it so that it ricocheted up to the second floor and smashed through a window. Then I rode away.

A while back, I told Nastiti that I might have been falling in love with someone. In response she gave me her sweetest smile. 'Do fall in love as hard as you can, while you can!' she said cheerfully, sincerely.

I will be wondering for the rest of my life. She swims through my head, one leg stretched out, her toes treading on the red-tiled roof of my boarding house, always so carelessly, as if she's not afraid of slipping. Sometimes she is a silhouette lying on a faux-fur rug in her own bedroom in the apartment, listening to Sigur Rós incessantly, absorbing all the song lyrics in an alien language that, according to her, told a story about a sleeping angel. At that point, she would close her eyes and the T-shirt she wore would rise to her navel. The men recognised her navel too, that mysterious vertical crevice. The men could map her navel like geographers. I myself had only seen it, along with a glimpse of the lace of her bra, on several occasions when she was neither conscious of nor concerned about my existence, and I hungered pitifully, simply trying to survive.

She reported, 'I found a condom in my mother's drawer. Who do you think she's doing it with?' Then she snorted. 'Never mind. Just imagining it makes me want to slit my throat.'

Nastiti talked of the men who surrounded her mother and cursed them with all her might. She came to me frothing with wrath or drenched in tears. 'Am I a bad daughter?' she asked. On that day, Nastiti had overheard her mother in the next room making love to a man, deep in the night.

'A place' was a bed-and-breakfast that I would soon search for so frantically that I missed it twice before I finally turned around. The front wheel of my bike almost hit a blue plastic rubbish bin that told us to put non-organic waste into it. Hours before, Nastiti arrived there with a familiar feeling of tightness. She brushed off the feeling — instead, she spent a few moments peering into the contents of that same rubbish bin to distract herself. Hadn't she once read a book with something like this in it? *It's surprising what kind of stuff people throw away every day.* Isn't that painfully true?

She thought about the rubbish bin.

Nastiti continued walking along the narrow parking lot at the front of the B&B, avoiding the leftover rainwater and mud trapped between the cobblestones, which was waiting to stain the jeans of anyone who wasn't careful. The place looked like an actual home, even though the meaning of 'home' to Nastiti for the past ten years had just been an apartment at the end of a long, tiled corridor that echoed all sounds. But here, she could blink and suddenly forget that there were strangers who would also spend the rest of the night behind these closed doors. It was a small street full of ordinary houses; it was nearly ten pm. The B&B was sandwiched between the houses of ordinary people who led ordinary lives. We came here to infiltrate those people's lives, to sneak into their beautiful and peaceful homes. Look at that place. From the window, we could see the top of a giant shopping mall in the distance and four apartment towers lined up, side by side, soaring into the sky. Nastiti thought of Singapore: that famous building, the Marina Bay Sands Hotel, with a concrete boat/fish/eel perched on top of its three towers; earlier, she had felt as if she were walking under it, along a lane that was full of potholes. In the reception area, we could see an old-style aquarium glowing blue-ishly. *Ssh*, the fish were asleep, floating between the bubbles generated by the water filter. On the walls were paintings of flower baskets.

Earlier, a security guard had greeted her at the gate,

somewhat annoyed because he was in the middle of watching a Serie A football match on his 14-inch tube television, Lazio against Roma, and the former was being brutally crushed by the latter (the security guard happened to be a fanatical Lazio supporter). A yawny receptionist asked Nastiti to show proof of reservation and payment from the website, which Nastiti had printed out and folded into a crumpled little square. Nastiti kept her mouth shut the whole time, and nobody asked anything important. 'Your room is on the second floor, left corridor.' The receptionist's smile didn't look sincere, but who cared? Soon she would end her shift, and she'd envisioned she would eat a bowl of instant noodles with corned beef and chili and then spend hours chatting on Facebook Messenger. Perhaps. She might also just sleep 'til morning.

'You don't bring any luggage, Ma'am?'

Nastiti shook her head.

'Breakfast will be available from half past seven,' said the girl, still with her toothy smile. 'In front of your room, there is a dining room, so you don't have to walk too far to have breakfast when you're ready.' The last smile. 'I wish you a good rest, Ma'am.'

Be my sister, Nastiti thought. In another life they might have been siblings, and this place would have been a real home with an intact, functioning family, as it was supposed to be. Nastiti clutched her tiny bag tightly as she accepted the key that the girl handed her — jingling and cold as it landed on the palm of her hand.

For a split second she felt the shape of her mobile phone inside the bag and thought of me.

She was prepared to find a simple, cold room, similar to a two-star hotel's or maybe even a hostel's, but her room was exactly like a normal bedroom in a normal house. It was both surprising and not surprising, and Nastiti couldn't help smiling as she took off her Keds and her socks, and then put her bare feet on the wooden floor. The soles of her feet hurt from walking so many kilometres. She threw herself onto the comfortable queen-size bed, spreading her arms wide, just like the Savasana pose she had learned in yoga class. As she took a deep breath, the air faintly smelled of synthetic lavender insect repellent.

The ceiling was low on one side. Nastiti wanted to stay curled up on that bed forever, until she died. She sighed, softly and insignificantly; her sigh escaped from a mouth that was barely open. A moment later she rose to her feet. She grabbed her tiny bag and dumped its contents onto the nearest table. She didn't stop to think.

She turned on the television, because she wanted to hear voices other than her own in the room, crying, perhaps, or perhaps not, and she turned on the damn television because she wanted to hear anything other than the frightening emptiness that surrounded her.

She had not forgotten. Her parents were going to kill each other. Little Nastiti hid in the bathroom, crouching inside the bathtub. The tap was fully on, but the level of the water was only just at her ankles. The wet part of her hair was tangled, tied with two rubber bands. She knew that Mbok Kum would later comb that tangled part with no mercy, and Nastiti shivered with anticipation of the burning pain on her scalp. She peered through a small opening between the wall and the bathroom door and saw that her father had taken a knife from the kitchen ... *Just do it, do it. (I'll kill you.) Do it!* Is all that real? Her parents were always fighting over things she couldn't understand, always, all the time. Nastiti had never known any other kind of parent, let alone the pair of laughing parents that she sometimes saw alongside her classmates at school on report card days. But she had long taught herself not to want what she didn't have. Let it be. She curled up, she played with the foam from her apple-shampoo bottle and ate blobs of strawberry-flavoured toothpaste straight from the tube. She would not stop playing until the storm was over and she could get out of the bathroom, and Mbok Kum would give her a clean white towel that was warm from the sun.

'Nastiti?'

'Hey.'

Her smile was beautiful. That girl, Nastiti, had a beautiful smile — she was a beautiful girl, but her smile would make you forget even *that* fact. You would simply be enchanted by her smile; you'd succumb to it. She was in the bathtub, staring straight through you. She wore a burgundy lipstick that stayed on even after she washed her face; the intensity of the colour didn't even weaken. That, and a pair of mascaraed lashes. The man didn't know much about women's make-up. He raised an eyebrow, smiled back at Nastiti, then, as if she were capable of telepathy, Nastiti raised a wet, slippery hand to her mouth and rubbed her lips until the purplish shade had faded away. The rain didn't come, the dark clouds had flown away, the lipstick was gone. Nastiti was soaking up to her chin in water mixed with liquid soap that was apparently made from goat's milk and nut extracts. Her knees appeared on the water surface like hills: erotic, dizzying. 'Come here,' she ordered.

'I thought you'd drowned or something,' said the man.

'If I die, I will tell you.'

'I thought you escaped through the window. Flying away like a superwoman.'

'Well. Didn't you hear me singing?'

'Yes ... but then it suddenly stopped. What song was that?'

Nastiti hummed through her nose. 'Don't you know that tune?'

'Absolutely no idea.'

'Geez, you're hopeless. How about this one?' She hummed again, this time a different rhythm. Her eyes were sparkling light-brown marbles. 'Come on. A hundred points if you get it right.'

'This is pointless.'

'Come on ... please!' The word 'please' was added after a pause, as if Nastiti wanted to sound more polite.

'What can I use these points for?' asked the man. 'Can I buy movie tickets with them or, I don't know, ice cream?'

'Even better. Still don't know? It's Mew. You know them?' The man thought Nastiti was talking about cats or some Japanese anime. But Nastiti went on to chatter about bands from Scandinavia with strange names; she was an active member of the fan club for this band, Mew. That earlier she'd sung a song called *Louis Louisa* and then another song called *Swimmer's Chant* ('Because I'm swimming, right? Swimming. Soaking. Whatever, haha'). She and her magical world, her love of alternative music, girls in trendy shoes, long wavy hair like hippies in the seventies, severely chipped nail polish. The man came over and sat on the edge of the bathtub while Nastiti continued humming in her high, sweet, bird voice. 'You could actually be a singer, you know,' he said earnestly. 'Help me scrub my back,' said Nastiti in return. They were in a hotel room, and nobody knew.

But of course, she told me later. 'You're crazy,' I said to her. 'Not really,' she responded. End of conversation.

She had made love to him many times without love, hadn't bothered with anything; she was in the bathtub, with him sitting there rubbing a bath sponge against her back, and then, *then*, of course, what could happen after that? She made love to him again, not caring about anything. I imagined her saying, 'You can exchange those points for a kiss.' And him, wide grin on his face, undressing himself theatrically. 'Come into the water,' said Nastiti. She never needed to ask twice. But who was that man, Nastiti? To me, they were all the same — just nameless and faceless shadows. The shadow was in the bathtub with her and making love to her in the water until her skin was shrivelled and grey, and then stood with her on the bathmat, water dripping from two soaking-wet bodies. They stood side by side in front of the mirror, bodies intertwined, together admiring their own reflection — they looked so in love, didn't they? Lately Nastiti had been losing weight, to the point of being as light as a bird feather. Her neck — which he nuzzled with a large beak-shaped nose — was streaked with blue veins, pulsating and warm.

'Where are you going after checkout?' Nastiti asked.

'Gotta go back to the office. I can only take half a day off.'

Nastiti realised that she and the man were hiding in that bathroom, in that four-star hotel room, as she used to do whenever her parents were fighting. Even though she no longer had a father and there were no longer fights in her house, she still found reasons to hide. She was still waiting for someone to greet her with arms spread wide when she came out of hiding, still waiting for the feeling of the dry scented towel caressing her skin.

'Hungry?' asked the man. Nastiti nodded.

They left the bathroom and released each other. Nastiti took a long time drying herself with a cold, heavy hotel towel, then she just sat on the messy bed, watching the man put on pants and a shirt from the neat pile in the cupboard. *Who are you?* she thought. After they had to check out from there, Nastiti didn't know where to go or what to do.

Now, she stepped into the en suite bathroom. There was no bathtub, thank goodness — just a rectangular shower box made of corrugated glass panels that took up much of the bathroom, along with a sink covered in decorative shells. There was a bottle of hand soap, and there was everything else that was clichéd, and there were various mirrors — Nastiti hated the versions of herself that stared back at her from all sides. She wanted to hide. A bathmat, very nice. She washed her hands in the sink after a bit of confusion regarding the taps, which, if you turned them to the right degree, would give you the exact water temperature that you wanted, so you didn't have to risk washing your hands with uncomfortably cold water. She took a scorching hot shower, urinated, then put a large menstrual pad into her underpants. The television was on, broadcasting the 24-hour news channel. Who wanted to listen to that kind of thing? The remote control was hiding in a drawer. Nastiti thought she wanted to watch MTV. At that point, she finally decided to charge her mobile on the socket under the table. She tore down her fortress to let a bit of the outside world seep in.

It was me. Nearly forty — or more? — of my texts flooded all of Nastiti's messaging and social media portals. Then me again, millions of missed calls before I gave up. One of the sadistic managers at her office had sent her threatening e-mails. Some of her girlfriends asked her something something (also some of the men, inevitably). Nastiti turned the volume up, and Coldplay started playing in the background. It was a song from their most recent album, *Ghost Story*, about someone disappearing. Nastiti had disappeared. At the same time, I noticed that there was now a 'read' sign on every message I had sent her. It was amazing that the signs were there, after who knew how long.

Nastiti approached the table. The time had come.

'I think this is a fun place. I think your mother must have loved your father very much.'

'Yeah, I think so, too,' I said.

'This Dara chick seems cool, huh. Cute, too.' Dara was my new girlfriend.

Nastiti flipped through a magazine, then she said, 'So,' and then she said, and she would always say them, those words, that had driven me crazy, 'so you know what? I'm not a virgin anymore.' Forever, that moment would stay there. I didn't know what to say. And then she said, 'You wanna know one more thing?'

'What?' My voice trembled a little.

'Hey, this is the first time you've ever invited me here, you know.' We had caught the train to my parents' house in Bogor on a weekend; the journey took more than an hour and we passed sixteen stations. 'Inside the train, it was like being in a can of sardines!' She shuddered.

'So, what was it like?'

Nastiti was interested in one particular glossy page that contained reviews of Hollywood blockbuster movies of that entire year — 2009, to be exact. She embraced the magazine like she would a cute little bunny. 'What was *what* like? Being in a train that was like a can of sardines?'

I clicked my tongue. 'Don't joke.'

'Oh. It only happened yesterday.'

We were twenty years old at the time.

'You really wanna hear?' she asked.

I was curious, but something in my stomach had fallen into a vortex. I thought of a heart that had detached itself from its stalk and plunged into a cauldron full of turbulent stomach acid. 'No, not really. You don't have to tell me.'

Later, at the beginning of the following week, at the bus station, I bought tons of pirated DVDs of the movies featured in Nastiti's magazine. I bought them all, together with two large packets of cheese-flavoured Cheetos and a litre of Coca-Cola. I phoned my girlfriend — she was working on her college assignments but was overjoyed that I'd called to ask her to watch the DVDs with me, as if I had saved her from some despair. We spent that night in my boarding room with all the lights turned off and the television on, sipping soda and eating Cheetos until our fingers turned orange. I set the AC to 16 degrees Celsius for my own disgusting purposes, and as I expected, Dara clung tightly to me under the blanket. I felt her toes slowly turn icy cold against my calf, then warm again, then cold again, one after another.

Nastiti — back to the Nastiti that was reading a magazine in the backyard of my parents' house — said, 'It feels like something has changed in me.'

'Mmm,' I muttered dryly.

The silhouette of her face was sharp and pointy against the last rays of the evening sun. I remembered that Nastiti's ancestors were Dutch, way back in colonial time, which explained her physical features. Then all the little details about Nastiti flashed through my mind, insignificant and irrelevant, but still I fell silent. *Guess what,* she used to say. *I finally kissed the guy. First kisses are overrated.* How many years ago was that? I watched her, how the ends of her hair fell, scattered, on top of the bonus poster of *Transformers: Revenge of the Fallen,* which I subsequently watched with Dara at the boarding house. A really stupid movie, full of explosions. *My* first kiss was with a girl who'd sat behind me in class, during the second year of junior high school. She was a girl with ordinary looks but a very pleasant personality. After it, my lips just felt sore.

Nastiti continued, eyes still fixed on the list in the magazine, 'I thought I wouldn't dare. I don't remember what I was thinking.'

'I was wondering why you were walking funny,' I said, meanly.

She looked up. 'Is it that obvious?' When I didn't reply, she spoke again, 'You see, it hurt.' I didn't want to know. *I didn't want to know.*

'Your dude's thing was that big, huh?' I resisted the urge to spit onto the grass. My mouth felt dry after a while of not smoking and having that torturous conversation. But Nastiti laughed, then the rest of her laughter evaporated into thin air.

And then, that ridiculous movie was already halfway through when I started shaking under the blanket with Dara in my arms. My thing stood up and she felt it, of course, but didn't pull away. I was still a virgin and couldn't guess the status of my girlfriend's virginity. But I saw that she closed her eyes and smiled an enigmatic smile (what's with girls and enigmas?). I was amazed and excited, and shaken, and angry at Nastiti for making me feel this way. But what could I do. I kissed Dara, I began with her slightly parted lips that revealed an orange tongue, then her neck, her ears. Dara tasted of salt even to my tongue, which was already numb from consuming too much MSG. I couldn't stop.

Nastiti had stopped talking altogether. She put down her magazine to drink from a tall glass of orange juice my mother had made for her. And she was right — when she moved, even the simple gesture of drinking through a straw didn't look the same anymore. Something inside her had changed.

'Are you scared?' I asked Dara.

Her gaze was filled with emotions I couldn't understand. (*I thought I wouldn't dare. I don't remember what I was thinking.*) 'I don't know,' she replied.

She was beneath me, and she was everywhere. Our clothes were scattered everywhere, on the floor in between the Coca-Cola bottle and empty Cheetos bags. 'To hell with it,' I muttered to no one. Then I entered her.

Instantly, down there, something was torn — a sheet of paper, a sheet of cloth, a flower petal that you plucked in awe of its softness, its freshness; an inexplicable slippery membrane, you found that a woman's body was an alien world, and you broke into it with all your might. I felt an intense sting of pain, as well as immense pleasure, so that I could not prevent my tears from pooling. My head was spinning. Dara was pushed to the wall, jerking. Again and again for good.

After that, we lay together, staring at the darkness that was stained with yellow and blue lights from my television screen. Beside me, Dara was sobbing or panting, or asleep and snoring. I didn't understand what those faint sounds meant, so I got up to clean the sperm that I'd purposefully sprayed on the bed sheet to prevent unwanted outcomes. Then I went to the bathroom, and once I was in there I didn't want to come back out.

We just never know. We wake up every morning and never know what will happen. For example, my father passed away in my arms as I was carrying him to the bed from the wheelchair, crossing several metres of distance that turned out to be a chasm between the living and the dead. Another example: it was still early in the morning and Nastiti's father perished on the highway. I didn't know, but the day I finally found Nastiti at the B&B would be the last time I'd ever see her. Could someone disappear for a second time?

Dara stayed with me for over five years — from the night we fucked at my boarding house until recently, until things got out of my control, and I found myself sitting at the dining table with her noisy extended family, caught in the middle of a conversation about our 'future' as a couple. I was so terrified that I was paralysed in my chair. Those people spoke in code, and my dying brain became a kind of search engine that was only able to catch key words: 'proposal', 'marriage', 'household', etc., etc., etc. Who decided all this and why didn't I fight back?

I had lost Nastiti. That fact engulfed me more than anything else. Then one day, for the first time in the rest of my life, I said it out loud. 'I've lost her.'

I spoke to the back of Dara's head; her hair swung as she raced ahead of me to the jewellery shop, where we were planning to order a pair of wedding rings. She liked white gold, not yellow gold. If possible, a single diamond. I stopped walking.

'What? Who?' Dara turned to face me. 'What are you talking about?'

'I'm sorry ... I can't go on with this.'

The wounded look on her face wounded me as well, as if it were slicing my throat. Even so, really, I admired her efforts not to embarrass us in the crowd that was swarming in the shopping centre, walking around us. She stared at me without blinking as tears rolled down her cheeks, but she bravely wiped them away and then she turned around, acting as if nothing had happened. Our five-year relationship made me understand that I had to follow her back to the car in the parking lot where we could continue this drama quietly, without other people listening in. It was there that she began to cry bitterly into her palms, as if she refused to watch me shatter in front of her. I loved Nastiti, and I had lost her. I didn't love Dara, and I knew I would lose her.

At the end of the day I was alone, tired, and vacant, realising that now I had nowhere, no one else to return to.

And at the end of a different day, we'd return to that bedroom and see Nastiti's belongings scattered on the table. She didn't stop to think. The pills were white and hexagonal, clustered at the bottom of a clear plastic bottle.

(*MIFEPRISTONE — also known as the abortion pill, RU 486, Mifegyne, Mifeprex — and MISOPROSTOL — also known as Cytotec, Arthrotec, Oxaprost, Cyprostol, Mibetec, Prostokos or Misotrol — are types of abortion drugs with a 97% success rate.*)

Would she need water? She didn't want to stop to think, because maybe then she would stop all this. She would focus on that 97%, even if it couldn't prevent cold sweat from appearing on her hairline.

(*With these drugs there is a risk of heavy bleeding. You should consult a gynaecologist immediately if that occurs.*)

She might die. If she didn't die, the foetus in her belly would. If she died, then both of them would. Nastiti reached for the clear plastic bottle with a sweaty hand. She had obtained the drug from an acquaintance who had access to the black market. Everything was blurred, blurred. Nastiti didn't care; the bottle was here now. The whole world was asleep except someone far away who was practising the piano. *How strange is this moment*, she thought. *Like a very long dream.*

All she had to do now was count the dose of her misoprostol pills until she reached a total of 2400 micrograms. That meant twelve pills to take over nine hours: four every three hours. It was past midnight now. Tomorrow morning all this would end. We'd witness Nastiti put the first four pills onto her wet palm so that, when the pills had gone, there were white marks on her skin that might have been real or might have been her imagination. The white marks were like traces of sin, like the blood of an innocent child.

(*Put four pills — containing a dose of 200 micrograms each — under your tongue and allow them to dissolve, do not swallow.*)

Another method, which they said could be more effective, was to shove the pills into the vagina. Nastiti had considered it. She sat on the bed, legs spread, her two fingers reaching inside to see how far she could get. But then she stopped, disgusted, and, instead, she slumped down and crouched on the wooden floor. There she noticed that there was absolutely no dust, no footprints. This floor was an innocent floor, there was no stain whatsoever, there were only her dirty shoes lying close together as if slyly whispering to each other: *Look at the girl, look at her.* The pills would creep up into her body from below and would slowly kill what was in there.

(*You will have cramps after two to four hours, along with some bleeding.*)

Nastiti waited. MTV aired an episode of some reality show. The person who had been practising the piano stopped. She waited, she sat down, then lay down, then sat down — then an hour, two hours had flown away, and the cramps came in waves that ebbed and flowed. Nastiti was standing on a beach, both feet on the sand touching the water. We know how it feels. We all have memories of playing on strange, unforgettable beaches, and those memories are eternal in the form of blurry and forgotten family photos. But we never forget our fathers in their ridiculous swim trunks, who guided us as our legs sank deeper into the sand. The ocean waves came gently, as if seducing us, and left silently. Our feet were sucked into the sand, and in Nastiti's case, she leapt, and asked for help, and called out, and grabbed any hand that offered salvation. Such family photos stick to my mind like the worst of my freeway nightmares. I had once found a photo in the Bogor house in which I was a kid on the beach and the waves were cloudy green under an ink-black sky (why black? Was it late at night? Or was the camera resolution just poor?); I floated, I appeared faded like a ghost in between the waves and the sky. Nastiti also had such a photo in her own house. We were all once kids at the beach. Yes, all of us.

... And the cramps returned, this time with a vengeance. Meanwhile I was calling her nonstop, so the rhythmic sound of Nastiti's mobile phone vibrating on the table seemed to coincide with the sequence of her cramps. Coming at the same time, going at the same time — it was music for dancing. Pulsating and wavering. Nastiti waited. I waited patiently to reach her by phone. *Nastiti*, I said to myself, *please answer*. She rose from her kneeling position on the floor and started pacing back and forth. Her feet made no sound on the floor but left damp footprints. Now the floor was stained, no longer without sin.

Then, after three hours had passed and I had given up my attempts to reach her, Nastiti went to the bathroom. There she pulled down her pants, checking the state of the pad she was wearing. She saw the first blotch of blood on it. Then she left the bathroom and went over to the table to get more pills. It was the second round. Her blood came gushing out.

(*Bleeding is a sign that the abortion process is in progress. The cramping and bleeding will continue to intensify and will peak after you take the second to third doses.*)

I went to the roof to smoke again, staring at my phone. I'd already triumphantly finished half of my second cigarette pack; the butts filled the ashtray near my feet. I would probably die of lung cancer before I was forty, so I picked up another cigarette and lit it, nonchalantly, almost without a pause, from the previous one. The smoke billowed onto Charlie, a half-blind feral tomcat who was always running rampant on people's rooftops. I had named him Charlie because he had a 'moustache' like Charlie Chaplin. I called out to him, but he ignored me. So, I looked back at my mobile phone screen, and at that moment Nastiti called.

Funny, right? Funny, because all at once I couldn't speak. But my ears caught her familiar voice seeping out of the phone — she sounded casual, although a little high-pitched — and it was indeed Nastiti. It couldn't possibly be anyone else. Here we'd catch strange vibrations as if from a missed radio signal. She said my name.

'Where are you?' was my question to her. *I've been looking for you since god knows when* was what I never said out loud. But, of course, she knew what was in my heart too.

So Nastiti answered.

I think we might have been communicating in a special dimensional space, a symmetry in which we understood each other perfectly. I heard Nastiti call me to come to her even though she didn't say anything like it. When the call was disconnected, I took my keys and helmet, jacket and handkerchief; the noise of my motorbike was deafening in that area full of boarding houses; it was almost four o'clock in the morning, but fuck it. The first thing you would hear is Nastiti calling you, asking for help.

The same security guard was still watching the TV, which was now broadcasting a soccer match of another league. A different receptionist welcomed me and didn't question me, even though I'd showed up at the place early in the morning for absurd reasons (were they trained for that? Not asking questions and not wanting to know?). Nastiti was in room number five. There was no doorbell or anything, so I knocked on the door for a while until I saw the knob turning and the door moving open, and the next thing I knew Nastiti was in front of me, standing unsteadily, and she said she was pregnant, and I saw her inhabit space and time as if she were inside a giant bubble, and I asked her, 'What are you doing? For god's sake, what?'

I will be wondering for the rest of my life. She swims through my head, and later that night, a blanket tangled around her body while she was shivering with a high fever, the empty pill bottle lying close to her on the pillow, her face covered in strands of hair. Her moaning stays forever in my soul, forever, Nastiti. No words, only moaning, groaning due to pain. 'I'm here,' I said reassuringly. 'I'm not going anywhere.' As usual I was there for her. Nastiti rolled over to vomit off the side of the bed, but nothing came out, and she cried silently; what came out was only her tears, flooding, forming an island of moisture on the pillowcase, and I wiped those tears with my handkerchief, but was there any use? Tears keep coming back, no matter how we try to get rid of them. What could I have done? I took off her jeans and her padded underwear. The pad was heavy with blood. I held her up, as if she were just a severed, shaking arm clinging to me; I carried her easily on many trips to and from that goddamn bathroom where she squatted on the floor and pushed out blood, and in the end we stayed there because she wouldn't stop bleeding ... Nastiti, what else could I have done? Maybe the sun had risen out there; maybe out there, people were already welcoming yet another day in their lives — days that repeated and multiplied so many times that we all ended up just running in a circle. On the bathroom floor, clots of dark-red blood flowed down the drain. Inside the bathroom, morning might have come and gone, but we didn't know it because of the disorienting illusion created by the white lamp, reflected on the white tiles and all things. The pale-white Nastiti was leaning on me; we were in a place where the earth didn't rotate, everything was white except for the splash of dark red that merged with the stream of water, then it disappeared and disappeared. I waited patiently. Nastiti's eyes opened wide, following the clots of dark-red blood that flowed down the drain. It was endless white and dark red. I waited until everything was over.

When it was over, I took off the loose shirt she was wearing as well as her bra. She stood there naked and wobbly, with both hands tightly gripping my elbows. I washed her: I turned on the hot shower, washed away the last remnants of blood, washed the sweat off Nastiti's body, drenched her wet hair, and it took all my strength not to cry. *Don't cry, you idiot.* I was an idiot because I could only cry until my own sadness suffocated me and I choked. But we got out of the bathroom, we went back to bed. Nastiti lay down like a sleeping angel.

I walked around the room. I went from one corner to another and didn't know what to do. I wanted to smoke but I didn't, even though I had never in my life had such an extreme desire to smoke. *Nastiti. Nastiti.* Without realising it, I hummed along to a video clip of a band playing on MTV. Nastiti was sound asleep, her breath going in and out of her nose and mouth in a soft, stable flow. She was fine. Her arm muscles twitched; a finger moved, once.

And out there, life would go on, because that was the way it was supposed to be. In here, I climbed up onto the bed beside Nastiti, inserting myself under the blanket, and she felt like a warm lump of cotton against my goosebumped skin (her fever had not subsided); she was delicate, breathing. I knew my own life had stopped at that exact point with her, while in my arms, under the blanket, Nastiti was plunging deeper into a sleep without dreams, dreams without core, and I wasn't there. In fact, no one was there. Here you had another muscle twitching, another finger moving (her index). You were processing the fact that those clots of dark-red blood had really been there on the bathroom floor, and all that could not stop itself from happening. You wondered why, how; your mind bombarded you with all the unanswered questions that would keep hovering over you, even when life had gone on, one year, five years, and the rest of your whole life that had yet to happen.

Three days later, a dead foetus came out of Nastiti's body in the form of a ball of blood the size of a marble that, at first glance, looked like a piece of liver. That odd, silken thing momentarily stunned her, as she realised that once it had had a life of its own and what could have been a beating heart. But because she didn't want to pause for too long to think, she immediately wrapped the ball in a soft cloth. She buried it in an empty lot far away from home, when no one was looking; it was a place that she got to by driving for two and a half hours one weekend. Life had gone on; she didn't stop to look back. The following day, Nastiti was able to wake up as usual in her own room. She went to the kitchen to eat yogurt with slices of fruit and found her mother ready to leave, smelling good, hair in a bun and in a full flight-attendant uniform. 'Where are you flying, Ma?' she asked as usual. Her mother answered: Perth or maybe Bangkok (one of them). Not far, but she would have to stay for two days (Nastiti remembered when she was a child and had loved to watch her mother create that spectacular bun whenever the opportunity arose). Then her mother asked if Nastiti was going to work, and she nodded. Oh, just like always, right? She selected a pair of pencil trousers and a blazer to wear to the office that day.

That was how Nastiti took her steps: she put one foot in front of the other without hesitation, tracing the path of life, never looking back. But she knew that, even if she looked back, she would find nothing. Nastiti woke from her sleep with a feeling of lightness that filled her like air. She laughed. She went on living because that was what she wanted.

I woke up and felt disoriented. When I looked beside me, Nastiti was no longer there.

According to the girl at the reception, Nastiti had left a few hours ago. What time was it now? Who knew or cared? Who cared about what happened to the both of us? The girl at the reception had drawn herself a pair of uneven eyebrows. She asked, very politely, if I needed anything. *No? Are you sure? No, nothing, I'm sure.* I left the place to get my loyal motorbike in the parking lot, realising that the day had once again turned into late night without me being aware. My head was spinning from hunger and from sleeping too long, but I had no interest in searching for food, even if I might die. I lit up a cigarette. Then I realised Nastiti was gone forever.

Being gone forever is as easy as: 1) just leaving, 2) deleting and blocking my name from all digital contact lists and social media accounts, 3) forgetting that I ever existed, 4) disappearing forever. And really, fuck it. So, I started my motorbike and left that place, riding until I reached a familiar area where I could clench my teeth as hard as possible behind a Shoei helmet, tighten my grip on the motorbike's handlebars, and ride as fast as I could along the Semanggi Interchange. It was almost empty, and I kept speeding along the road, avoiding the few cars that were there (I was like a crazy person), until I arrived at Jalan Gatot Subroto: office buildings and hotels and malls lined up on both sides of the street. Even if suddenly there would be police, fuck it. I rode my motorbike with earbuds booming heavy metal music into my head. Don't do what I do, kids. Now, where were we? Jakarta flew past me with the speed of a bullet, so I could only see brilliant-coloured lines in my limited field of vision through the helmet's visor. I loved those streaks of flashing light with all my heart. I lived in it. I was running away, Nastiti.

That same night Dara answered my call with a happy tone. 'Heyy, you out there? Haha, why?' So that was that. I waited in front of her house — her fence was distinct, and was always mentioned to mailmen, couriers, or distant relatives who were visiting so that they could easily find the address. She came out to meet me, her face full of happiness. 'Hey, what's up?' she said. I realised I hadn't showered or eaten since who knew when. 'Wanna go watch a movie?' I asked. We went to the midnight screening at the cinema, then ate at a nearby 24-hour fast food restaurant, where I gulped down a large hamburger and two pieces of chicken breast with rice. But that time was long gone.

Here we are today. Dara sounded like she was in a cave when I called her, a few weeks after I ended our engagement. Despite everything, she still picked up after only three rings, as if she were looking forward to it. For some reason. Then I said, 'How are you?' She was silent, so I waited, smoking a cigarette, listening to the noises in the background. Dara was on a busy street. Impatient people were honking their horns, bus attendants were screaming at the top of their lungs to attract passengers. 'Where are you at?' I tried again.

'On the street, waiting for a cab.' The cab was approaching, and I heard her get into it, greet the driver kindly, and tell him her destination. She was not far from where I was now. So, I asked, 'Care to meet?'

'Why?'

'Because I want to know how you are.'

'I'm going to Loretta's. We're going to hang out.'

'Then after that.'

'Would take a while; it could be until late in the evening.'

'That's okay.'

She was silent. Then again, 'But why?'

In the end, we agreed to meet at our regular Starbucks. I found myself sitting comfortably in the cafe's corduroy chair and, since we'd almost always chosen the same spot each time we went there throughout our relationship, my chair seemed to remember my anatomy quite well. Dara and I sat face to face; at first, she kept looking in the other direction — basically anywhere but at me — but in the end she turned to look at me, finally. She appeared healthy and her skin was glowing. I thought she'd spent the last few hours having a good time with close friends. *That's great.* I said it out loud.

'Retta won a scholarship to study a master's degree in Europe. That was our farewell. She'll leave this Saturday.'

'Are you alright?'

She smiled. When was the last time she smiled at me? 'Yes. I guess.'

'I reckon they hate me now. Your friends.'

'They do. But it's okay. How are you?'

Me? Just like usual. Work in the mornings, out with my friends in the afternoons, cigarettes in between. It seemed like this was how most of us lived. Some other lucky bastards, meanwhile, could go abroad to go to school again, or shoot a movie, or open new restaurant franchises. 'I'm fine,' I said.

She sipped her cold mint tea out of a *venti*-sized glass dripping with condensation. I watched her drink, then take a bite of a blueberry muffin.

'You're a good liar.'

'Well, okay, it's true that I lied a bit. But you do look good though.'

'It's because I've accepted all of this. That we're done.'

'You hate me?'

She nodded. 'Initially.' It was amazing how that big glass was already almost half-empty, after only a short while. 'But not anymore.'

'Yeah? Why not?'

'I feel sorry for you. That girl, Nastiti. Where is she now?'

I chuckled. 'She just ... left. She left me. And I'm done looking for her.'

'Oh, dear. Poor you.' And she seemed genuinely sorry for me. I felt sorry for myself. I was proud of her, my girl, whom I had failed so terribly.

'Do you want to hear the full story?'

'Did I ever *not* want to?'

'Please keep this a secret.' She nodded. 'Promise?'

'Promise.'

I told her everything, without holding back. She listened to me attentively. Just like in the past, her hands were clasped under her chin; she didn't talk while I talked. It was pleasant, relieving. Just like peeling off a scab. I realised she remained silent when I had become silent. My story ended.

'Dar?'

'Yes. What?'

'So that's all.'

Aren't I such a mess? I didn't say it, but she shook her head. Then, 'Dara?'

'Yes?'

To be honest, I couldn't bear to lose any more people. Dara looked at me directly, still sipping her tea. I realised that she was still wearing the thin gold necklace with the tiny heart pendant that I had bought for her a few years earlier — it was silly, fake gold, and Dara had dipped it in nail polish so that, she said, the gold colour wouldn't turn black too quickly due to oxidation. I realised that I *did* love her, but not in the way I loved Nastiti. I loved her because she was someone precious, a close friend, a sister, someone who always understood. What is love, anyway. What does love mean? Maybe I would never be able to start any kind of romantic relationship with Dara again, but I didn't want to lose her. This time I said it out loud.

'I don't understand you,' she muttered. Then, 'I'm still your friend.' She held my hand on the table and squeezed it to give me reassurance, and we smiled at each other. At the boarding house, after that, I opened my laptop and deleted all the photos, videos, documents, voice recordings, anything related to Dara, because from now on, things would be different. Then my pointer moved on the screen to do the same exact thing with everything related to Nastiti.

What innocent creatures we are — we never know the meaning of a pile of memories that are crammed into a certain span of our life, and furthermore, we can never guess how long that span will be. Someone can come into our life so easily and go just as easily. One day, Nastiti was there; for years, we slid down the same slide and peed in the same toilet bowl at school, and she left when I thought she was somebody who would always be in my story. But if this were a book, Nastiti's chapter would be over.

It took me a very long time to be able to come to terms with it — that most of the things in the world are beyond our control, and Nastiti is just one example. Do I love her? Yes. Did she love me? No.

Yet there was something else, something different about her this time, like a room where someone has thrown out all the flowers while you were gone: a change in the interior you don't even notice at first, not until you see the stems sticking out of the garbage.

HERMAN KOCH
THE DINNER (TRANSLATED BY SAM GARRETT)

RUKMINI

They were alright. They moved on and tried to forget. Sometimes they celebrated their forgetting by buying new furniture, like a dining table — large and a total eyesore, dominating the entire dining area — or sculpted teak furniture from Jepara that seemed to cost my father his entire two-month salary. They bought cans of wall paint in a dramatic dark colour and decided to remodel a bedroom or bathroom, and then, months later, they regretted it. They put new light fixtures on the ceiling and planted all kinds of new plants in the garden — winged beans, lilies, allamanda — as well as tiny cacti in pots that lined up on the veranda (don't forget to evacuate them into the house if it rains!). They were forgetting. When it became too hard to forget, they tried hugging each other. These were the words they whispered to each other: *It's okay, hush, we're alright.*

You're alright.

My mother was the one who needed to hear it the most, although she would never tell my father that. But he would give her those words anyway. I grew up watching them whisper to each other in various corners of the house, watching my mother sit quietly in that carved Jepara chair in the middle of the night. There she was, my mother, under the dim light of the streetlamp that snuck in through the window — I would see her on the way to the bathroom, after I was awoken by my bladder, afraid that I would wet the bed. At first, I thought she might be a ghost and I almost screamed, but then I realised it was just my mother. There it was, her figure, light and dark, in a batik negligee she had bought one time in the Malioboro market when we went on a family outing to Yogyakarta long ago. She would just sit. Gradually, I got to know my mother who lingered in the middle of the night, she who was a ghost. She did it so often that over time I would get up on purpose to secretly observe her, that ghost who was my mother. I imagine there was a hot drink steaming in her hand. I imagine her drinking it.

You have served me a cup of this warm drink, which looks delightful in this cold weather. Look at that steam billowing up into the air. You're also being very kind by providing a jar of chocolate cookies that I understand will be opened once for me to take one, and then be put back in the cupboard. At least, that's the kind of anecdote about Dutch people that we hear in my country. It feels strange that I'm saying all this, because actually I have a little bit of your blood as well in my veins, and I know, when you look at me through those square-rimmed glasses, you are unconsciously trying to find these Dutch features in me. I don't know if I have them, although to my eyes, my mother always looked very western, so maybe I do too. But I've never really known your country and I understand that I am not one of you. So I smile at you, a little nervous maybe, and you say, in a fluent but careful — almost academic-sounding — Bahasa Indonesian, 'Please do have a drink, Ibu.[1] How was the trip from Jakarta?'

Should I tell you that I woke up just before my plane was due to land at Amsterdam's Schiphol Airport at about half

---

[1]   Ibu/Bu literally means 'mother' in Bahasa Indonesian, but in formal situations, it can be used to address woman.

past eight in the morning, with a lingering nightmare looming above my head? The freeway and the void, my husband's body lying on the side of the road, and my long-dead mother saying, 'Hush, it's alright, Arini.' I woke up with a kind of spasm. 'Did you sleep well?' asked Maria, who was passing by, followed by a junior who looked a little frightened. 'The office said you were on long leave, so I wondered what was going on. It turns out that you're vacationing in Europe, eh?' She said all that with a smile. Should I tell you that Maria was my batch mate from cabin crew training, millions of years ago? It has indeed been a million years, just flying before our eyes. Suddenly we are all old.

'It was good and smooth, thank goodness,' I reply. I reach out to the table and touch the small plate that you have put there for my chocolate cookies. There are also two sachets of artificial sweetener of a brand I've never heard of.

'Do you come to the Netherlands often, Bu Arini?' you ask.

'Maybe once every two months because of work,' I explain. 'I've never stayed long. Usually we leave again to another destination in Europe or Asia and then return to Indonesia. The technical term is "layover". Or we go straight back to Cengkareng — I mean Soekarno-Hatta Airport — after a day or two in Amsterdam.'

This morning my plane had landed on the runway with the usual thump. I went through all the long procedures of arrival, immigration (everything was painfully slow); I waited for my baggage, I waited. Schiphol Airport consists of wide corridors bathed in gloomy grey light that barges in through various spheres of glass. November is almost over, and the world will welcome the dreaded December in a few days. This morning I wrapped a new scarf around my neck — so new that it still had the price tag (I forgot to take it off) sticking out of its blue wool fibres. The airport: where my whole history lies.

45

Airports are my second home, where, almost on a daily basis, I'm used to walking at a fast pace over the tiled floors with a large suitcase on wheels, the wheels rolling smoothly, my heels tapping, people glancing at my uniform and bun, glancing at all of us (usually the cabin crew walk together in a small group, while the captain and co-pilot are a few metres ahead, chatting among themselves). No one has ever realised how tired we always are, as all our emotions are skilfully hidden behind our smiles and heavy makeup. But this morning I looked around with teary eyes. I looked at a large middle-aged man who rushed past me, then watched a little boy with long, curly hair keep trying to run away from his mother, who was sitting at a Starbucks, having a breakfast of sandwiches and coffee. Now, looking back at you, I want to say that I'm thinking of my own daughter. At home, Nastiti is probably dreaming about her final high school exams, which will happen soon. I imagine my daughter waking up and finding a message from me under the Eiffel Tower–shaped magnet on the fridge door: *Mami went to Holland. Will be back next week. Your favourite cake is in the fridge.* She will only shrug and not make a fuss.

Then you suddenly say, interrupting my daydreams, 'I hope you have had enough rest at the hotel, Ibu. Every time I visit Indonesia, the jet lag is terrible.'

'Please, uh … just call me Arini,' I tell you.

You smile and ask me to do the same with you — calling you by your first name — which I do with relief. We call each other by our first names. The pleasantries go on, and I'm a little surprised when you pull out a recorder, turn it on, test it, and, when you're satisfied, put it on a table next to me. I glance at you. Maybe a confused look appears on my face. You smile again, and this time it is an apologetic smile.

'For my archive,' you explain.

I nod, hesitating a little. 'Okay.'

'Shall we start?'

I nod again. To my surprise, you leave the cookie jar on the table, so I can grab some any time I want.

Semarang, Dutch East Indies, March 1942.

They found my mother hiding under a table that the mistress of the house used to compose her personal letters. Not long after, they also found my mother's older sister from a different mother, from Mevrouw de Witte, the mistress of the house. My mother's sister's name was Engel. When they found her, she was standing stiffly in the middle of her bedroom, just below the crystal chandelier, because she didn't know where to go or what to do.

She was still wearing a pretty red dress after a friend's birthday party. Was it true that their father was screaming *Run, run*? I have no idea. But Dai Nippon's army had arrived, just as it had been warned for weeks on the radio and in the newspapers. In the yard, there were several others standing guard in front of a military truck, its engine still humming. My mother knew they would be ordered to go into that vehicle and would then be taken away somewhere. Engel's mother recited the Three Hail Mary Novena. Their father, Meneer de Witte, looked defeated but determined. My mother frantically looked for her sister's hand in the tangle of outstretched bayonets and menacing sweaty arms. Time passed like an eternity, and the novena did not stop even for a second: *Holy Mary, Mother of God, pray for us sinners now, and at the hour of death*, resonated in the depths of my mother's soul while the truck roared its way down the hill, leaving their house in Bukit Tjandi, Semarang, heading for somewhere. *Where are we going?* asked Engel. No one knew.

The truck was already packed with plenty of their white neighbours and other Europeans who lived in several other parts of the city. My mother recognised one or two of her school friends. One person quickly became motion sick and coughed and threw up on the truck floor; the vomit splashed on the shoes of the person sitting next to him. Now Engel's mother recited the Lord's Prayer: *Our Father who art in heaven, hallowed be Thy name, Thy kingdom come, Thy will be done.* In the future, even to the end of my mother's life, the words of that prayer would haunt the most beautiful and the worst of her dreams. Act of Contrition: *I am heartily sorry for having offended Thee, and I detest all my sins because of Thy just punishments, but most of all because they offend Thee, my God, who art all good and deserving of all my love.* At some point she had to stop, because her streams of prayers annoyed the Dai Nippon soldiers, but Mevrouw de Witte managed to find a way to continue even with her mouth shut. She sobbed, she begged God for forgiveness. My mother and her older sister held hands all the way, and time stood still for an eternity.

Dai Nippon soldiers took them to a detention camp for Europeans — Ambarawa internment camp 6, I think. You can check the number later, because there are several of those camps in that area. What I'm sure about is that she would stay there for nearly three years, until a Dai Nippon high-ranking military officer chose her to be taken to another place, which was just as bad, if not worse. Like her mother, my mother became something like a concubine. *Jugun ianfu*. But I guess you know a lot more about the term than I do, don't you?

The envelope had a sender address on it: Gerard Doustraat 156–1075 VY AMSTERDAM, Nederland. The address was electronically typed and printed on the label, but the letter itself was handwritten — very neat and italicised, using a slow-drying gel-based pen.

'Mother?'

She sat with her back to me. After her death I often saw her sitting with her back to me, in my dreams, sitting as still as I had always seen her in life. That day I would fly to Europe — my first European assignment. We still lived together. Then I got married, so I left her alone to care for my father who, on his 56th birthday, had his second stroke.

'Ma?'

She showed me the letter. The contents were in Dutch, which I did not understand.

'What's this?'

'A letter from my older sister's son. Engel — she passed away last week.'

'What?'

I started laughing, but immediately remembered that my mother rarely joked. There may have been periods in her life when she was being funny, or even joking, but they must have happened long before I existed. Or perhaps they never happened. I fell silent. I looked at her. The letter shook slightly in her hand.

'Ma, you have a sister?'

'Yes. Her name is ... was Engel.'

Engel. I remember that, at that moment, the name 'Engel' echoed with a vague majesty in my mind, resembling the word 'angel'. It wasn't until much later that I learned that the name actually meant angel in Dutch. My mother's older sister was named an angel by her European mother, while my mother was named after her Javanese mother. It wasn't until years later that I learned all about it, slowly and piece by piece, because my mother wasn't psychologically prepared to explain everything in one sitting.

'Ma, what are we going to do?' I remember asking in desperation.

'Where are you going?'

'Europe ... ah, the Netherlands.'

She started crying. It was all so odd. I stood there not knowing what to do, towering over my mother, who sat crying in a completely different way from how other people cry. She looked straight on while her tears fell, as if those tears had a will of their own and my mother's body couldn't fight it. I was ready to leave, in full uniform and already carrying my suitcase, and I froze, not knowing what to do.

'Give my greetings to Engel when you get there,' said my mother at last.

A few days later, when I arrived home, I came to her. 'Ma,' I said, 'it's for you, chocolate from Belgium.' I felt nervous when I said it because I didn't know anything at all.

So you say, 'Jugun ianfu.' You say it slowly, as if you want to know how the words taste — bitter or sweet or maybe both. In one of my haphazard investigations into your background (before I agreed to any of this), I found that you were also fluent in Japanese. This is your area of expertise: the Indies, Japan, the Second World War, studying all of that. It seems so long ago and distant, almost unreal. I imagine you wandering amongst the traces of the atomic bombings in Nagasaki or Hiroshima, and I imagine you talking to the locals in flawless Japanese. Roaming around. Digging, snooping. There is a twitching on my tongue; I want to ask *why* you do all this, but my question is swallowed into my throat along with a sip of the warm drink. It turns out to be coffee. I don't drink coffee.

'Jugun ianfu,' I say, nodding. 'When I first heard the term, I felt ...' Why would *you* care about how I felt? I'm out of words. 'Eh ... it felt extraordinary. There could be no way all of that really happened, could it?'

'Unfortunately, it really did happen,' you say.

I nod again. 'That's why I'm here, right?'

You smile. 'As we agreed, neither your name nor your mother's will be mentioned.'

'I know.'

'The term means "military comfort women". There are a few other terms, of course, but this term is the one we use widely.'

'I prefer to translate it as "Japanese military comfort women",' I say dryly. I clear my throat. 'Any other meaning feels wrong. It was the Japanese who created their existence. I read a little — these women were everywhere, in all the places they invaded. The women. Including my mother.'

I shut my mouth as if I had just blurted out a swear word. 'Oh, God,' I sigh. Oh, Mother. Help me.

Witte means white in Dutch. You might think this is ironic. As a child, my mother had inspected her fair skin and wondered what made it so different from her own mother's skin colour. Now you too want to know about the woman. 'My mother's mother?' I say. 'Oh, she was a mistress.' I don't know if it is appropriate to call her a *nyai*. Probably not, because her father — the father of my mother — also had a legitimate European wife. My mother's mother initially worked in the kitchen of her future lover's home, as a cook (this kind of story took place everywhere fifty, a hundred years earlier, but not so frequently in those days). She was so beautiful that Meneer de Witte fell in love with her. But was it really love? Probably not.

My mother was conceived out of wedlock after several passionate but hasty encounters, in the kitchen near the sooty stove, or in the bathroom, or the vegetable garden, or in the shed, or even in the bedroom that belonged to her master and his wife. My mother was born white, grew white, with big brown eyes and hair the colour of peanut skins. Her mother was allowed to remain at the master's house to breastfeed my mother for some time, but then at some point, Mevrouw de Witte asked her, in a kind manner, to leave. Of course. It is possible that this story is inaccurate, but it is all my mother could remember.

She also remembered other things: the saffron-brown colour of her mother's arms, the tanginess of her body; the tall white people looming around her while she was running between their legs (there was a dance party, perhaps), *rijsttafel*[2] banquets a là Indies, going with a *bediende*[3] to buy groceries at Johar Market in the morning and seeing a big barrel filled to the brim with frog thighs, and pig snouts and pig intestines hanging from long rods. She remembered her father's Fiat. The black paint was sparkling, the horn blaring. Every Sunday they went to Mass in that car, every week without fail, because Mevrouw was a devout Catholic. My mother would receive communion — the wine and bread, the blood and flesh of Christ. Over time, Mevrouw became a loving mother to my mother, as if she had been her own.

She remembered her older sister. Engel walked, or walked

---

2   a meal consisting of variety of dishes
3   servant

fast, or ran ahead of her, the hem of her skirt fluttering, always ahead. But while running she also took the time to look back and laugh, and her teeth were white and neat. *Come on*, she would call (they were always together). They exchanged words in Dutch, which my mother understood until her death, but which never came out of her mouth again. The last Dutch words she spoke to Engel were *Where are they taking me? Waar brengen ze me heen?* From then on, they would never be together again, and my mother felt the Dutch language stabbing in her throat like a thorn.

'She was there a long time,' I explain. 'About three years, if her memory can be trusted. Nobody had a calendar back then.' My mother said that living in that deepest part of hell, the Ambarawa camp, felt like an eternity, although of course she had not yet experienced the hell called *ianjo*: the jugun ianfu brothel. But look, it seems you have a rather impressive binder with photos of the Dutch East Indies internment camps, and you show them to me while pointing at people and naming dozens of landlords, plantation owners, a bank director, and employees of colonial government offices — they who had been interned at various camps across the country. To be honest, I'm not really listening so the names just pass me by. The photos in the collection — in addition to the fact that they are all copies — look blurry and sepia, or very faded black-and-white, and perhaps were taken by somewhat incompetent photographers. I am daydreaming. One by one, I gaze at each of these pale faces staring back at me through the long stretch of time and place and generations. These assemblies of women and small children and gloomy teenage girls. Where are they now? I imagine them here in Holland, in a lovely little house with the curtains wide open and the heating on. They could also be dead. I guess you're in the middle of telling me which ones are alive and which are dead, to the best of your knowledge, but I don't really listen. The faces haunt me enough.

In my mind, I am pasting my mother's figure into your photos. In my mind, she is also present in various scenes of scooping water, lifting buckets, squeezing herself among other sunken-eyed interned people on a thin, perforated mat. Sitting up or lying down. My mother was very young: she was thirteen years old. She said that shortly after arriving there, she had her first menstrual period. Menstrual blood leaked through the back of her skirt and soaked the mat, disturbing the sleep of the other camp inhabitants.

A eulogy:

I sipped my tea, which had quickly become lukewarm. I knew that day would become a date on the calendar that I would silently mark in my heart, every year and forever. My fingers hugged the paper cup of tea that I'd bought in the hospital cafeteria. *Nastiti doesn't like tea*, I thought randomly. Then the nurse's voice gave me a jolt, and I almost jumped out of my chair. 'Bu Arini,' said the nurse kind-heartedly and in a gentle tone, 'we should go in. Bu Rukmini asked for you.' I knew that what she meant was that my mother's time on earth would not be long. She passed away that afternoon.

Then it happened again, like déjà vu. 'Bu Arini, your daughter is inside.' I wondered if the nurse was the same, if she was actually a messenger from the afterlife or an angel of death who was assigned by God specifically to take care of me. The hospital corridor looked like it was spinning around me, so the nurse vanished for a moment and returned with very sweet, very strong tea in a paper cup. I was still wearing my flight attendant uniform. My suitcase was still next to me like a loyal dog. After that, my sweet nurse took me to see Nastiti. She was lying on a patient bed with her male friend whose name I couldn't remember. 'Papa died,' said Nastiti. I waited for a while, until I was strong enough to see my husband's corpse in the morgue.

After that, believe me, I became an expert at composing eulogies. All her life, my mother always put us before herself. She always prioritised the interests of her husband and of me, her daughter, above her own. All his life, my husband was a responsible man, he always took great care of us, his family. Such words just flowed through my pen onto a piece of paper. I cried a little while writing a eulogy for my mother. The second time I wrote one, for my husband, I felt broken. I made sure to close the door of my room so that I didn't have to see Nastiti on those two occasions — she would know what I really wanted to write.

Almost all her life, my mother was a stranger. She was a ghost with flesh and blood, haunting me. She never loved me.

All his life, my husband was married to a woman who didn't love him.

I come out of my reverie. You look at me with concern. 'I'm sorry,' you say. 'Let's take a break. All this information must be overwhelming to you.'

I fix my gaze on the recorder on the table. I say, 'Nastiti is not her father's daughter.'

Whenever my mother cried, tears would fall down her cheeks just like that, as if she were leaking, and then the lack of liquid would deflate her. But whenever she told me about her past, I got the impression that she was actually bleeding so profusely that the blood formed a flood, and I was drowning in it. Sometimes I felt like running away from that flood of blood. I also needed to save myself, you know. I could go clean up dinner scraps, for example. I could tell her that I already had plans with someone.

Of course, in the end I would remain glued to my chair, staring at her without blinking, listening to her bleed before me. After a lifetime of questioning things by myself, I finally understood the mystery — *our* mystery. I came to slowly understand what had made my mother the person that she was, and why I was so unhappy.

I guess that had been her way of declaring her love for me. She opened up, then she left me.

Nastiti is not her father's daughter. You blink, perplexed, because you don't even know that Nastiti is my daughter's name. 'Sorry?' you say. 'Sorry,' I respond. The accident that killed my husband on the freeway crosses my mind, even though I was not there at the time and therefore it was impossible for me to see it. But like the tip of a sharp blade, the image still incises a deep, bloody wound. Now *I'm* bleeding slowly in front of *you*, even though you can't see the red.

'Ah, let's just rest, shall we?' you kindly offer. I love your blue eyes. How both eyes are very transparent and full of honesty. I don't answer because I'm imagining the blood on the asphalt, and my daughter who *was* there to see it. I swallow hard and nod. While you're taking me on a quick tour around your home, introducing your family to me, my legs go numb, as if it were I who'd bled out. But it's my husband who is dead, and I killed him. Nastiti is not his daughter. Nastiti isn't. I told him the truth, and he was killed in a car accident. It's so easy to kill someone who has loved you.

I'm telling you, even my mother had killed somebody. Maybe that capability runs in our veins.

When we return to the study, I ask you where in Amsterdam Gerard Doustraat is. Is it very far from here?

I still have the secret correspondence between my mother and her family that had been lost: letters that are neatly tucked away in my room in a drawer that is always locked. She never contacted anyone in the Netherlands by phone, so the only way to contact them would be by post, which I have never done. But the idea of meeting them has been on my mind for a long time.

'I believe it's not that far from the city centre,' you reply. 'So, about an hour's drive from here, I mean from Leiden.' You can guess what I want to do.

'I think now they're aware that my mother is dead,' I say. 'There were some new letters coming even a year after her death, but they will never receive her reply again.'

'I will take you there, Bu Arini,' you say.

I reply, 'They were looking for my mother for two decades, trying to trace her whereabouts through a series of contacts in Indonesia. And they found her. Now I want to find them back.'

Your recorder still sits on the table, like a small beloved pet. It is on again now; it rustles as if it had a life and could respond to your commands by jumping or barking. You are being so kind and careful with me. You are not pushy. You are not trying to steer my messy raving in the direction that you want, but rather you leave it as it is. Every now and then you fill in the gaps I create by providing statistics or other historical facts, or by citing a scientific article by somebody. You mention names. 'There is Mardiyem in Indonesia, who gave the first testimony about her experience as a *jugun ianfu*. Two years earlier, in South Korea, Kim Hak Soon started this movement, and she was the first to remind us that they *did* exist.' These two names I have known from my readings, but most of the other names I have never heard of. Just like my mother, no one in the world knows about their existence.

Then you go on to mention some Japanese names. 'Most of them were given Japanese names when they entered ianjo,' you explain. Those names. Mitsuko. Kazuko. Momoko. Mamiko. Momoye. Haruye. Sakura. The Japanese turned them into other people, complete strangers even to themselves.

My mother told me her name was Hana, which in Japanese means 'flower'.

My mother's last day as Rukmini went as follows:

The smell of something boiling filled the air. It was always humid indoors, of course, especially when it was scorching hot outside and the mevrouws were boiling something nasty for the interns' weekend meal. What was more, they were celebrating something — there was a malaria epidemic, but that day nobody had died (they didn't know what would happen tomorrow).

My mother and Mevrouw de Witte stayed as far away as possible from the celebration. Instead, they waited for Engel in a makeshift hut set up to accommodate malaria sufferers, about ten metres from the main camp. In the hut they were able to whisper to each other in Dutch, which was not supposed to be used at any time in the whole camp, but at that moment, my mother was not talking to the Mevrouw. She only heard the low hum of Latin that was her stepmother's prayers. If she was not praying, she did not speak. She simply arose from the mat when required, worked, didn't eat, then slept again. She had stopped wondering about her husband's fate in the men's camp, only God knew where.

They no longer counted the days, months, or years. They had no idea how much time had passed, but it should have been long enough. Since she first arrived at the place, my mother had grown a lot taller; her clothes didn't fit anymore (including the clothes that the Japanese had distributed when they were still generous), so that sometimes she switched clothes with Engel or waited for hand-me-downs from other interns. This time she was wearing Engel's short dress while Engel was wearing my mother's top and skirt. Now Engel could even fit in children's clothes. There was almost no more flesh on her body.

It surprised my mother how much had changed, and how much had not changed at all. Interns came and went. Diseases came and went. Little children grew up to be young girls and boys (although when the boys turned thirteen, they were immediately transferred to other camps), and very old people, one by one, met their end. Engel, on the other hand, shrank back into a child. Japan, meanwhile, did not leave the Indies. People said, out there, a terrible war was raging. In Europe, the Netherlands had long fallen under the rule of Nazi Germany. This is another World War, my mother kept reminding herself.

But the war felt so far away when my mother's focus was concentrated on her older sister, who was dying. Engel had shown signs of malaria just two days earlier. In the last twenty-four hours her fever had run very high, and she was shaking so hard she rolled off the *dipan* they were sleeping on. For the last three hours she had been lying shivering with her eyes closed, like a corpse, my mother thought, if a corpse could shiver. Then she thought again, with all her might as if it would be of use — *Hang in there, Engel*. She didn't pray. It had been a long time since she'd stopped doing that.

Her stepmother muttered a prayer.

My mother wondered why Engel had contracted malaria while she herself had stayed healthy, with nothing lacking, even though no one had been eating properly for a long time. But there she was, despite the situation, managing to stay in good health.

Suddenly, her stepmother stopped praying. There was a sound of an unfamiliar truck approaching from a distance. Even Engel opened her eyes for a moment.

'Maybe someone is coming with medicine?' my mother suggested.

They would soon find out (as you and I already know) that the Japanese would not bother wasting money and time taking care of epidemic victims in internment camps around the country. Later, my mother would tell me about that day, herself lying sick on the verge of death while I hesitated to take her hand, or do something sentimental, anything, but I soon realised that my mother didn't need the touch, in any case. My mother wanted to stay strong to the very end. Alone.

And that day they immediately saw that the truck was filled with Japanese soldiers from other units. The trumpet sounded, a sign that all camp residents had to gather in the yard. A Japanese soldier came over to tell my mother and the Mevrouw to *move, hurry*. The tip of his gun barrel was suddenly perched on the nape of my mother's stepmother.

But my sister is gravely ill! my mother protested in Malay.

The Japanese nodded his head towards the sick bed. *She's coming too*, he said. He meant Engel, of course. At gunpoint they went to the yard with Engel sandwiched between them. Engel's arms, which clung to my mother's neck and shoulders, burned like a steamed sweet potato that had just been taken out from a pan. Suddenly, it occurred to my mother that she was hungry. She thought about that imaginary sweet potato. Then she worried about Engel. Then she thought about the soldiers who had just sprung out of the truck in the yard.

I interrupt my narrative to drink big sips of coffee. I want to ask for water, but I feel uncomfortable asking. Silence. I blink as I notice that you have turned on the table lamp right next to me. The light is very soft and pale. How comfortable and dim your workspace is. I want to go to sleep.

Then you save me from having to continue. For my sake, you interrupt again with more historical facts from books. You talk about the recruitment process for *ianfu* throughout the Indies — some were scammed into it, some were persuaded, kidnapped on the street or forcibly taken from homes. Some had previously worked as prostitutes and did not mind spending wartime as Japanese harlots. But my mother ...

You, Rukmini de Witte, come here, was what she heard, and from then on, her fate would only get worse than it already was.

(I just made this up, of course. I don't know exactly what the Japanese said when my mother's name was called. She only remembered that she missed hearing it the first time, so someone smacked the side of her head. *You. Hey, it's you!*)

One after another, my mother recalled the young and beautiful faces lining up in front of her and behind her after an expressionless Japanese called their names from a fairly long list in his hand. 'Engel de Witte too?' you ask. Yes, her too. But Engel swayed and fell to the ground. They checked her and seemed to reach the conclusion that *this one is at best near death, will be troublesome, so leave her here.*

The process didn't take much time, even though the list was long. Without her realising it, the time had come when my mother had to leave.

The faces of young women surrounded her, *indo* and *totok* — mixed and full European — blooming and beautiful as flowers, even after their long years of suffering in the camp. They rebelled and struggled, or they quietly succumbed to their fate. For my mother, the most important thing was to see with her own eyes that her older sister was alive. Engel collapsed to the ground but was able to get up again.

Waar brengen ze me heen? my mother asked her older sister. Engel stared at her in despair. Meanwhile, my mother's stepmother sank into the melée that was starting to break out. She didn't appear to be anywhere.

The next day my mother was in a different place, along with the other women who had been chosen. Now she was Hana.

Dinner is a typical Indonesian meal — beef rendang with small round potatoes, white rice, fried red chili sambal, fresh vegetables, and fruit for dessert. I find myself sitting between your husband and your teenage son, who seems bored and sleepy, yet is friendly enough to me. You cooked all of it. I'm impressed. You look proud.

'It's not too hard to get ingredients for Indonesian cuisine here,' you explain. Of course, this is the Netherlands. 'We buy them from a toko. The word "toko" in Dutch means a supermarket that specifically sells imported goods from Asia.' This time we are chatting in English so that your family can be involved. In my language, of course, 'toko' just means a shop.

Your rendang is extraordinarily delicious. I tell you that sincerely, then I add with honesty that I wouldn't be able to cook beef rendang, because I have never made anything more difficult than instant food. My poor daughter grew up eating dishes made by our household assistant, Mbok Kum, or food that we would order from a restaurant if we felt like it.

'I fly too much,' I say, somewhat defensively. But nonetheless, using the word 'fly' gives me a strange sensation of freedom. I'm a bird that can fly! I pity those who can't fly!

'Tell me more about your daughter, if you don't mind,' you say with great interest.

'Her name is Nastiti.' Where do I start? She is a beautiful child, so beautiful that it worries me. Beauty like that can sometimes destroy your life, like what happened to my beautiful mother. 'She's a ... complicated child.'

'She pretty?' your son jokes. Asks to be introduced to my daughter if she is indeed beautiful. I grin. I want to confess that I don't know her very well.

This is my fault: I have run away from my daughter, the way my mother ran away from me. I desperately want to say that, but I keep my mouth shut. The dinner continues in peace. Then it's time to drink something warm in front of the electric fireplace (coffee for you and tea for me), and then it's bedtime, and you guide me to the sofa bed in the middle of your study/library. I welcome my sleep with gratitude.

It's just that I keep having nightmares. I wake up at two am and, made worse by the jet lag I rarely have, I'm unable to fall asleep again until dawn.

The Netherlands.

Now everything looks different to my eyes. Being here feels

different. Perhaps, almost like coming home. I don't know how to explain it, but I hope you understand.

My mother never came here.

'I wonder why?' you ask. I shake my head.

'I guess she just didn't want to.' I don't know.

'So, Engel de Witte survived malaria and made it through the war.'

'Malaria saved her from having to be a jugun ianfu,' I add.

We are at the park near your house, taking a morning walk. We have been chatting all morning. When we are in a public place, you don't bring your beloved recording device along with you, but you never forget to bring a small notebook and pen. I'm talking and you are taking notes.

By late morning you promise to take me to The Hague, to the governing capital of this country, so that I can witness the legacy of my people, which I may have missed on my previous visits: remnants of the Indies, and what has survived that remains to this day. Most of the white colonists who were sent back to the Netherlands during the war chose to live in The Hague for generations, you say, and according to letters from my mother's family, they also settled in The Hague — at least, until Engel's two children decided to move closer to Amsterdam for work.

'So Bu Rukmini was never here,' you say.

'No, never. She never saw the ships that evacuated the Dutch people sail away from the Indies. She didn't know how to find out about the fate of her family. My mother thought they were dead.'

'When, in fact, they didn't die,' you say.

'Data belonging to the Japanese military showed that my grandfather died in the camp due to old age, exhaustion, and malnutrition. Engel and her mother survived. They left for the Netherlands in December 1945, then started a new life, here. Mevrouw de Witte never remarried; instead, she entered a convent. When she was twenty-two years old, Engel got married, and later gave birth to two children, a boy and a girl. It was all in the letters from Engel's son. I translated it with the help of a sworn translator.'

You take notes.

'Then Engel died. Even for that, my mother didn't want to come to the Netherlands.'

'Was she angry, sad, disappointed?'

'Her dead sister wouldn't be able to recognise her again, that's why,' I answer. My mother, I will never be able to understand her.

The Dutch East Indies.

In my mother's eyes, her older sister was a real angel, a seraph, a true embodiment of her name. *Ruk! Listen up!* She had been very beautiful when one day, shortly before the war, she burst into my mother's bedroom; very beautiful when her cheery steps — as cheerful as if her slippers had springs — suddenly came to a halt and she became hesitant; very beautiful when a moment later her doubts magically vanished, and she jumped up to occupy the vacant space beside my mother on her bed. She was very beautiful. *Listen to what, precisely?* my mother asked. Before the war, they were famous in the Tjandi area as the beautiful de Witte sisters. My mother put away the book she was reading. *Yes, Engel, what's the matter?* Engel smiled at her; she smelled like an arm full of flowers freshly picked from a garden, mixed with the fleeting scent of sponge cake and talcum powder and sweat. My mother was fascinated by her older sister, ripe and mature, seventeen years old, who knew the world in a way my mother did not.

That night Engel talked, giggling uncontrollably, about her first kiss with a French man who worked as an accountant in their father's estate office. *He's older, of course. Hush, shut up, shut up, don't be too giddy, Ruk. Yes, very handsome. He has a handlebar moustache. It tickled a little when he kissed me. Oh but ...!* My mother couldn't sleep. The words 'first kiss' carried over into her dream. The following weekend, the two of them attended morning mass at church, and then, somehow, Engel disappeared for a few hours. Later, she was back in her own bedroom after dusk, and my mother found her lying on the bed, facing the window. My mother walked over to her. *Engel?* she called. Engel cried softly. *I have sinned*, she whispered. What sin?

Now my mother understood that sin was a French man pulling up your skirt and pressing you against the wall while his mouth moved to kiss your neck, yet you let it happen, and you loved it, and you gasped when he broke the locked gate to enter your body, yet you enjoyed it. That sin was a Japanese soldier who didn't even put down the gun slung over his shoulder while he took away your chastity, yet you didn't snatch that gun off his shoulder to blow his brains out and then your own.

It was not your fault, Mother, but you still felt dirty and guilty all over your body.

Early 1945. The end of the war was far away. The house was still filled with Dai Nippon's military, and that day was the beginning of the third month Rukmini was there, and she was bleeding from the rectum so incessantly that, for that day only, she was separated from the Japanese soldiers who were lining up to enjoy her body, and there she was in a room at the very back of the house — a place where occasionally a girl was taken to die — and from your room you would hear screams, cries, screams. Then nothing. In the end there was always nothing, rising from that back room like a stench that you could not smell but could feel. Each time it happened, Rukmini would sit huddled in the corner of her room and would think, *one more*, then a few days later there would be one more, one more, and you'd be wondering when it all would end. *Janneke jumped out of the window of her room, she plunged into immortality before landing in the yard with a loud thump, and it sounded like a sack of potatoes dropping on the ground, she's dead, she must be, her room is very high.* This time for just one day, Rukmini was free from all that, but she was not free from the smell of the men's saliva that still stuck to her mouth and nose, the unbearable pain in her groin, the shortness of breath from the men's bodies that had pressed against hers. She wanted to cry but didn't, because could there be any use? What would be the point of crying? She closed her eyes so that she could see nothing, but could there be any use? A Japanese doctor came in and examined her, then applied a strong-smelling ointment to her bleeding rectum. The pain was excruciating, and Rukmini wanted to scream, but could there be any use? Instead, she tried to focus on a memory: one day, on Bodjongweg, she and Engel had bought fries and chipolata ice cream at the famous Toko Oen, eating in a corner next to a large vase full of withered paper flowers. They had smiled, looking at themselves in the mirrors that covered the wall — everything was still alright, wasn't it? She remembered being happy, that the ice cream hadn't melted in Semarang's hot weather but had been quickly demolished by their two greedy teenage mouths, and the fried potatoes had been cut in big pieces, Belgian style, yellow and greasy, and they had tasted like heaven. Rukmini closed her eyes, but she knew that another girl was being brought in because she could hear her voice, followed by the voice of a *pribumi*[4] woman who muttered to herself in low-class Javanese, which she remembered being used by her own mother who had been a bediende; it was the language of the *djongos*[5] and *baboe*[6]. Rukmini opened her eyes. The Japanese doctor moved to the side of the other girl, who had been laid on a bed a few metres away from Rukmini, and held the girl's thin wrists firmly so she couldn't struggle too much. 'Yoh, do it,' the doctor told the pribumi woman in Malay. The girl turned to look at Rukmini with her blue eyes.

She was pregnant, that girl — Rukmini could see the small hill that was her stomach. Sometimes this happened, and the girls would be brought here to have their babies die. The pribumi woman was the one who did it. She was an *orok*[7] shaman, some sort of traditional midwife, a village massager who was summoned to carry out this terrible task for a banknote of Dai Nippon Teikoku Seihu rupiah. Now the girl was pleading with her eyes. Maybe she just did not want to be alone. She didn't ask for help. So, Rukmini looked back at her. *You are not alone.* Before she knew it, the shaman had started to massage and squeeze, massage and squeeze, and the girl was howling. Rukmini watched the girl's tears and blood spill. Rukmini was frightened but did not close her eyes, because she needed the girl to know that she was not alone. She must be strong. *Hey, hey, shh, you are not alone. We have to be strong.*

---

4   native Indonesian
5   lackey / male servant
6   (in colonial time) female pribumi who worked for European families to take care of their children; (modern) rude Indonesian word for household assistants
7   Javanese: infant

Rukmini fought back her tears. The smell of blood swept into the air, the blood from her own anus as well as the streams of blood that were gushing out of the girl's crotch. Now the girl had passed out. Horrified, Rukmini watched as a small lump of bloodied flesh fell onto the orok shaman's waiting palm. The baby died. The deed was done.

Jakarta, 1989. I showed up late at the door of my childhood home in the Kampung Melayu area, carrying a fabric carry-on suitcase that I had bought on an assignment to Beijing — it wasn't the trolley case I carried on the plane for work. That, along with a tiny bag filled with lipstick, wallet, and Yves Saint Laurent hand cream. My all-knowing mother let me in without asking. Without saying anything, she boiled water to make a hot drink, and then, to my surprise, she also started heating oil in a frying pan, and took out pieces of seasoned chicken from the refrigerator. She had prepared turmeric fried chicken, my favourite. Sitting opposite her at the dinner table, I found that I didn't have to hide my emotional turmoil because my mother wasn't paying attention. That was fine; it was normal. 'Eat,' she said. Before me was a plate of steaming hot rice. I nodded. 'Can I stay the night, Ma?' She turned towards me, observed me carefully this time. She nodded. 'Eat,' she said again. The chair I was sitting in used to be occupied by my father, until his death many years ago (stroke, of course, plus its complications). I'd never imagined how lonely it must have been for this woman. I took one fat chicken thigh. I took a full spoon of rice.

But before that mouthful of rice entered my mouth, I had an unbearable bout of nausea. Suddenly, the turmeric fried chicken looked like a piece of leftover food that had been thrown into the rubbish. The smell was unbearable. My mother watched me without speaking. 'Ma, I just need to sleep, is that okay?' My mother nodded. She knew, because she always knew. But she would never say anything.

A few hours earlier, I had run away from the house I shared with my husband. The day before, I'd had a big fight with him over a phone call from a man, and he'd slapped my cheek so hard that I fell onto our bed. The week before that, I had flown out of town, with the man who had called, who'd been the first officer on my plane. A month earlier, that man and I had had sex in his house, when his wife was out of town. Three months before that, we had met for the first time and had fallen in love. Today, I was feeling nauseous and almost vomited at the sight of my favourite food. I knew I was pregnant. My mother also knew, because she always knew.

What I didn't know was that, as she stared at me sitting there, clenching my mouth to hold back vomit, my mother was thinking of the blue-eyed totok girl who lost her baby, long ago in wartime. She did her best not to think about her own life, but she couldn't help it, could she? I didn't know all that, because I never did.

So, she still didn't say anything. She cleaned up my untouched food and led me to the room I had occupied for years, as a child, then as a young woman. She brought me a tube of rubbing balm. A moment later, she went to bed.

Seven months after that, I gave birth to my daughter, Nastiti. My mother did not come to see me at the hospital.

'I ... remember,' I say, my entire mouth bitter, as if it were full of sawdust. *Like the taste of your mouth when you are pregnant in the first months, everything is bitter and sickening.* 'I remember. I was four years old. I was on a swing in a nearby playground one morning. I quickly became engrossed in it. Before I knew it, I had swung as hard as I could and accidentally let go of the swing. As a result, I was thrown several metres away, landing on the gravel. My parents were there — *Bapak*[8] ran towards me, he was panicking, dead pale, but was still adept at wiping the blood from my wounds. It hurt so much. I was crying uncontrollably. I wanted my mother, but she was far away, sitting on a park bench with her hands neatly folded on her lap. Just staring. She didn't come to me.

'Then I was in junior high school. I had my first period, and I was terrified when I found blood in my underwear. I didn't know what to do. I was too embarrassed, too scared to ask my mother for advice. The blood soaked through my uniform skirt while I was in class. No doubt my classmates laughed at me and were still talking about it a week later. At home, I cried all night in my bedroom. It was my father who came to comfort me. He was the one who taught me to stuff a small, folded towel into my underwear and showed me how to wash it. When I had cramps, Bapak made me herbal drinks to relieve the pain.

'I remember that my mother was always at a distance. There was only my father. Photographs of Bapak cuddling me, bathing me as a baby, taking me to school, teaching me basic math. He took care of both of us, my mother and me, even though he would always love my mother more.

'I once asked him if his wife had ever loved me. *Of course*, he said, *she loves you in her own way*. I was too embarrassed and afraid to ask my mother the same thing directly. Until she said it herself, and slowly uncovered her dark past for me to understand. So that I was willing to forgive her.

---

8 Indonesian: father

'In the end, she was desperate for God's forgiveness, but I reckon it's God who should ask forgiveness from her.'

The Japanese man had no name. People just called him the Commander. They were afraid of him — the low-ranking Japanese soldiers, the pribumi lackeys, you name it, everyone was afraid of him. He wanted Rukmini. The girl had become well known in Dai Nippon's military circles for her beauty, and it was for that reason that he wanted Rukmini for himself. And who could say no to him? He was the Commander; they were all afraid of him. So one day, she did not know the date, Rukmini found herself being taken away in another military truck, heading to another place. Before that, she had been cleaned, though inadequately, and the usual doctor had separated her to be examined and treated, to make sure that she was free of dangerous venereal diseases. Then she was taken away by two soldiers. She no longer looked back, nor did she look forward. She just sat there, looking at her fist on her thigh. She tried not to think about anything. She would be alright. Everything would be alright. She would grit her teeth and endure everything. Hadn't she survived this far? *Engel, are you dead? Does God exist? Did Our Lady convey the prayers that were offered to her?* Rukmini didn't look out the window. People would look at her and wonder why she was flanked by a pair of armed Japanese; she hated windows and everything they could show her. However, she was back in the outside world at last, and the window proved it. It was daytime. This was the city she knew and loved. This was not a fever dream. In fact, Rukmini wasn't sure exactly where she was, but there was no mistaking it — this was the city that she loved. They drove back into Semarang. She raised her face and peeked at the world outside through the window that she hated. The wheels of the military truck rolled over the gravel road. They rolled along the Konijnenstraat, she was sure of it, and she saw several bare-chested pribumi men walking in single file, followed by a Japanese soldier or two. Japanese soldiers patrolling on bicycles. Japanese soldiers everywhere. Barefoot pribumis, stepping along the gravel paths. Rukmini lowered her face again. I don't know for how long. Then, they arrived at another house. The house used to be owned by a happy European family, but they were now imprisoned in an internment camp somewhere. So, the house had belonged to the Commander since the war began, and the country was now in ruins. While a soldier held one of her arms tightly to keep her from running away, Rukmini planted one foot on the bottom step. What would happen to her? The Commander was waiting at the top of the stairs. *Welcome*, he said in Malay. Rukmini didn't want to look at him, but the man grabbed her chin. *Look at me.* Their eyes met. He was handsome. He wore a full Japanese military uniform with ranks shining, reflecting the sunlight. Rukmini tried not to think. She would be alright. Everything would be alright. She would grit her teeth and endure everything. She didn't fight back — it wouldn't do any good. Hadn't she survived this far? She didn't come here to die. If she resisted, the man would kill her, because that was the way they did things. That man could do anything to her. She didn't care; there was no way she could be any dirtier, more despicable than she already was. So she let the man take her into the coolness of the high-roofed rooms with colourful tiled floors. He gave her a white dress, similar to the one Engel had liked to wear to Sunday masses. Rukmini would let the man do it: give her a dress, lead her to a bathroom with white tiles, strip off Rukmini's dirty clothes. The man bathed Rukmini with his own hands, shampooing her hair, lathering her body with soap, scrubbing off the dirt, pouring water on her, rinsing her, drying her; how gentle his movements were, as if full of love. Rukmini watched the water flow down the drain. She was completely naked, then the man took her to a room, where he put new underwear and a bra on her, then the rimpled white dress, the hem falling exactly half an inch above her knee. The man combed her hair, put lipstick and scented powder on her, then, when he was done with everything, told her how beautiful she was. He told Rukmini to turn around so he could see her, but Rukmini did not do it. The Commander didn't mind — he didn't become angry and go berserk brandishing a weapon, like some of the lustful soldiers in the previous house would do. Instead, he approached her and embraced her. One hand began to touch her body, reached under her dress, touched her breasts, played with her nipples, twisted them with his forefinger and thumb, gently, as if full of love; he kissed her face, crushed her lips, his tongue pushed into her mouth, the man sighed and groaned, and Rukmini was paralysed with fear. But she would be alright. She just needed to endure it a little more, and what would be would be. What could be worse than this, anyway? She could have been lying dead. The man lay her across a large bed. Rukmini wanted to cry but didn't, because what would be the point? Now the man was taking off his own trousers. His cock was already hard, erect, like the flagpole they'd planted in the ground of the internment camp, under which the Dutch were occasionally punished, made to stand and sing *Kimigayo*, their song, before being flogged. Slowly, as if full of love, the man covered Rukmini's body with his own, and, in an instant, he entered Rukmini while sighing and groaning. He stabbed her again and again while his groan became louder, until he grunted and then stopped with a jolt.

Rukmini didn't want to cry but her tears betrayed her, flowing out like the man's semen flowing into the cavity in her body. And she found out that tears and semen were the same. But the man could do this, right? Because Rukmini was only a woman.

'*Commander*,' you say, half-musing. 'During that period, Central Java was still under Major General Nakamura Junji, commander of the Japanese Empire's Sixteenth Army, but in Semarang the garrison was led by Kido Shinichiro. Both men's military title was "Major". Could it be that the Commander was Major Kido?' Then you appear to lose yourself in your thoughts.

'Sorry, I don't know,' I respond. 'Maybe not that high in rank.' Why is this important? But I see that you are just curious, a typical academic curiosity.

'How long was Bu Rukmini held captive by him?'

'My mother was lucky — she only spent two or three months with that person.'

My mother thought the man was not actually bad. He was not cruel like the others. His soul was just tormented, like the others.

'If the Commander was an influential top military officer, it's possible that he was killed in the Five Days' Battle two months after independence,' you say.

My head hurts. 'Maybe,' I reply curtly.

My mother could not possibly be aware of it, but out there the Japanese occupation was almost at its end. In there, meanwhile, she didn't realise that she had stopped menstruating. She was sixteen years old.

Later on, she would be thirty-four years old when she became pregnant again: with her only daughter, me. She would be in a safe and secure home, with a husband who loved her unconditionally. But this time, my mother was a Japanese man's mistress — she couldn't go anywhere, she was locked in a big house that was guarded by four soldiers from morning until night. She had to have sex with the Commander in the morning, before he left for the army base, and three times in the evening, when he returned home. Sometimes the Commander talked to her in Malay. Occasionally, he even talked about his wife and children back home, calmly and with melancholy.

Now you are my wife, Hana, the man told her.

Then, as Japan's position sank further on the world war map, the man's attitude changed. He began locking himself in the study for hours. He also touched my mother less and less.

One evening he just left the house and never came back. My mother was pregnant with his child but didn't know it yet.

You: 'So what happened then?'

Me: 'My mother. She killed her own baby.'

Semarang, 18 October 1945. Five Days' Battle.

Rukmini wasn't aware of the battle, had no clue about what was going on around her, because no one bothered to tell her. Because she was alone, because she had no one, because that's how life was.

The Commander suddenly disappeared. Rukmini woke up in the morning and was surprised to find that she was alone in bed. She immediately realised that there was something wrong with the house, so she left the bedroom and checked all corners of the house. There were no more servants and guards. Was she free? She wasted no time. Since she'd had no belongings for a long time now, she only changed into clean clothes (men's clothes that had belonged to the Commander — an oversized linen shirt and trousers) she found in the cupboard, and quickly slipped away through the back door. This time the door was unlocked, of course. She tiptoed through a small half-tended garden, almost falling over a rubbish bin that had tipped over, lying on the ground. She let out a small laugh of disbelief. Then she started running.

Then she ran. Then she ran. At first it felt easy, but after a while she had to force every fibre in her body to run, run, run. The last time she had heard her father's voice was when he told her to run. So now she would keep running, even if it killed her. She was barefoot, and once or twice a piece of sharp gravel or broken glass pierced her sole, but she didn't stop. Shouldn't. October. Two months earlier, independence had been declared in Batavia, but Rukmini did not know. Now, the country was no longer the Dutch East Indies. Semarang had been liberated from Japanese rule. Beyond Rukmini's knowledge, real chaos was happening everywhere; Japanese soldiers against pribumi youths, pribumi youths against the Dutch. On October 14, the first day of the Five Days' Battle, the pribumi youths captured thousands of Europeans outside the internment camps and threw them in prison. Things were not safe for an Indo-Dutch girl wandering the streets with no direction. However, Rukmini did not know that.

She had one destination in mind: Tjandi. The sun began to rise high above her head and made all the gravel, rubbish, sand, twigs, and asphalt beneath her feet scorching hot, burning her skin. She was still running, though she'd begun to stumble more and more. She was parched, she wanted water like never before; the bleeding wounds on the soles of her feet from stepping on all kinds of objects were being roasted by the heat of the road. Rukmini was crying but she didn't know that; her tears just fell, flowing down her cheeks as if they had a will of their own. From then on, this would be the way she cried, her body had forgotten any other way.

Noon. Eventually, she stopped looking for street signs and began to try to identify directions based on mere memory — familiar road bends, for example, or odd-looking house roofs, a mango tree that did not bear fruit, grocery stores (now out of business), Protestant churches attached to boarding schools for girls. Wide roads that began to slope upwards. Up ahead, she knew, she would reach Tjandi, which had been her home.

It was just luck that she always managed to find a shadow or a piece of wall to hide from strangers. And her life remained attached to her body. Isn't God good? A little longer, Rukmini. She only stopped once to vomit in a bush, but nothing came out, of course, only a trace of soured saliva. Then she ran and ran again until, all of a sudden, she had fallen on her knees in her own yard, looking up at her own house, which was now abandoned. Isn't God kind?

She cried for some time and then passed out on a bed of dry grass.

Even after all that, she survived, my mother. It was pancreatic cancer that finally took her life, at the age of seventy-three, two years after the turn of the millennium. She spent a week in intensive care, and she breathed her last with her daughter by her side.

At the age of seventeen, she took the life of her baby son.

Indonesia, October 18, 1945. Someone saved her. A pribumi, but not somebody from the nationalist youth group. She was just a widowed woman named Minah, who happened to be passing by the former home of the de Witte family, on her way to somewhere. There she saw a young girl in men's clothes lying on the ground, so she rushed over to the girl to check whether she was alive or dead. A white or indo girl, she thought, still breathing, though rather weakly. Minah used to work as a bediende in a Dutch house nearby, and her master's family also had a very beautiful girl, like this child. The woman was feeling my mother's body, touching here and there to wake her up. She found that my mother's lower belly was swollen. *Pregnant*, she thought, *about two to three months along*. She hurried back home to ask for help. That day the widowed woman saved my mother's life.

October 20. In and out of consciousness for two days, kept alive by drinking starch water and eating pieces of steamed cassava, my mother woke up on a strange bed in a strange house. A voice speaking Javanese — *ndak apa-apa, Ndok, cah ayu*. It's alright, little miss, you beautiful miss. After a few more days, my mother learned to fully trust the pribumi woman who had accommodated her, and when she became strong enough, she tried to help out any way she could as an expression of gratitude. Early the following week, a young man, who turned out to be Minah's nephew, appeared at the house to inform them of the arrival of British troops on Java. That man would later become my father.

October crept into November. The chaos died down, then there were other flare-ups here and there, then they too died down, and no one could predict what the next day would bring. But time seemed to go faster; strange, wasn't it? Mid-

November, and my mother was too afraid to leave the house. My future father, who knew someone from the nationalist youth group, was reporting regularly about ongoing incidents. Extensive fighting broke out in Surabaya. More and more white nations' military troops came to extort independence from the hands of the people. My mother huddled in her safe little room for days, shivering.

She knew that she was pregnant with the Commander's child. Time passed, and her belly was getting bigger and bigger.

Your father knew about the baby? your voice floats from the depth of my subconsciousness. *Yes*, I reply. My mother told him honestly about the fate that had befallen her. How lucky she was that he still loved her, loved her half to death.

November to December. At the end of 1945, the Dutch began to leave the former Indies in large groups, including my mother's stepmother and sister, but she didn't know that; she thought they were dead. Then the new year began. My father-to-be got a teaching job in the capital: *Will you come with me, Rukmini? Would you be my wife?*

I am here now telling you about our family's secret to atone for my mother's guilt. But as well as that, I want to atone for my own guilt, to tell you my own secret. Who would guess? Just like her, I also gave birth to a child who was not my husband's. My husband who died in a car accident some time ago. An accident that I caused.

My father waited a month for an answer. My mother accepted the proposal, but her pregnancy was now very far along. She would give birth in a matter of weeks.

You have been pregnant. You know what it feels like: we walk around and travel around, moving from place to place with the baby in our bodies. We are never alone, we always have someone to accompany us because the child, the baby, clings very tightly to the wall of our uterus. Suddenly, the world is filled with only that child and we, the mother. The two of us, really just the two of us.

My mother, she moved from place to place with the illegitimate baby she didn't want clinging to her like a parasite, dirt, like seeds of cancer. The bigger the foetus, the more alone she felt. Please understand, she was only seventeen years old. When my mother died, she begged me to understand, and I understand, I forgive her. Since her death, I keep thinking about my mother, who had spent the rest of her life begging the baby to understand, but there would never be an answer. Maybe right now, in the realm of the afterlife, she is still looking for the child she killed to ask for forgiveness.

1946. What month didn't matter. My mother knew only that there was an unbearable pain down there, a pain she never imagined could exist. She would later find out that it was April, the month when around three thousand Dutch troops landed in Semarang to begin preparing for aggression. Meanwhile, on the other side of town, after six hours of labour assisted by Minah, my mother gave birth to a baby boy.

He was such a perfect baby boy.

Minah told my mother, *Ndok, ndelok iki anakmu bagus tenanan.* Look at your son, he is so handsome. The man who later became my father was also with her. Even though his heart must have been torn apart, he didn't say anything; instead, he moved close to her, he wiped the sweat from her forehead, brushed the wet hair from her eyes, held her close. He took the baby, and he swayed him. He sang a song. Don't cry, oh my, oh my, don't cry. *Cah bagus.* Shhh shhh. Look at your son, Rukmini. He also wanted to say, don't cry, Rukmini, but didn't say it out loud. The baby was still crying, so was my mother.

One week passed.

What do you remember from the days after giving birth? I remember the pain all over my body. Swollen breasts throbbing, legs still swollen, and sleepless nights due to having to breastfeed with both swollen, throbbing breasts. I remember paralysing guilt. All the pain that wouldn't go away, both mental and physical. Meanwhile, my mother remembered falling into a dark abyss and being trapped at the bottom for a very long time.

And she was still in the depths of the abyss when on the eighth day, she approached the basket where Minah had put the baby to sleep. Unconsciously she began to sing very tenderly, an old Dutch lullaby, *Aan d'oever van de snelle vliet/ een treurig meisje zat* — in his basket, the baby was breathing softly, his nose twitching, producing a very faint birdsong — *Het meisje huilde van verdriet/omdat zij geen ouders meer had*. It was exactly midnight, and you could hear a large bird screaming out there, up in the sky, like the screaming of a human being in agony, but Rukmini's baby boy was a little bird. *Aan d' oever van de snelle vliet/een treurig meisje zat*, a gloomy little girl/sitting by the river. *Het meisje huilde van verdriet/omdat zij geen ouders meer had*, she was crying due to grief/because her father and mother had gone away.

Rukmini held her breath. She stretched out one hand, slowly, one finger touching the baby's warm, paper-thin skin; tracing the curve of his cheek, his two closed, slanted eyes (the eyes of a Japanese); his two big ears (the ears of a Dutch); and finally, the slope of his flat nose (the nose of a Javanese); and Rukmini closed her eyes tightly. She closed her eyes tightly until there was only darkness covering everything, then her hand moved, and clamped his little nose, little mouth, his warm cheeks as thin as paper, die, die, die.

Your voice, low: *Did he?*

Yes, the baby died.

Mother, here I am now.

In front of me, the road is almost empty, but it's still quite early in the morning. I sit on the right side of the car while my new friend drives on the left. I'm tempted to tell her that sitting on the right side in a moving car, and on the wrong side of the road for me, still gives me the impression that we're going to crash. Horrible. But I stay silent, because I'm not interested in small talk. Besides, of course, she would hear my heart pounding. So instead, I just watch the bicycles go by. Not so many bikes yet, Ma, because it's still quite early on a Sunday.

The sky is grey. There are red, brown, or grey buildings on both sides of the road. I can vaguely hear my new friend explain about construction projects in the Netherlands over the past decade, occasionally pointing out a house or building and telling me about her favourite restaurants, or shops where she can buy cheap winter coats and snow boots for climbing the Alps. *The French part of the Alps*, she laughs, *because the Swiss part is too expensive. Everything's too expensive there. Ha ha ha.* Surely she has the right to joke a little after we tormented ourselves with the ending of your story. That dawn, Minah found them both. My mother told her the baby was already lifeless when she checked on him. *Maybe because of some disease, angina or something, I don't know.* Her face was without expression when she said all that. Deep down, Minah could guess what had happened.

Oh yeah, Switzerland is really expensive! Ha ha.

We head for Amsterdam from my friend's house in Leiden. I'm holding the address — written on a piece of cardboard torn from an empty cereal box — in my hand. Most of the journey is spent on the motorway, until, almost an hour later, the car finally turns into the city of Amsterdam, then into the Oude Pijp area. More people start showing up on the streets, more bicycles, so many that I come to believe that the number of bikes here is greater than the number of people. Our tyres roll over the asphalt road, and then the grey-brick road and tram tracks.

It is not difficult to find the address. You never had the opportunity to see it, Ma, but this place is so beautiful. The canals are beautiful, the boats on the canals and rivers are beautiful, too, and there are beautiful old bridges that cross over these canals. We park on the side of the road near the canal. Then we walk a little bit until we arrive in front of the house of the son of Engel, your sister.

I honestly don't expect anything, Ma. I even consider turning back for a second, but after taking a deep breath, I continue moving forward. The house is a three-story brick apartment building, with black-framed windows. Gorgeous. We stand at the door, and I ring the bell. *Ding dong*.

Five minutes later a tall, bespectacled middle-aged man opens the door for us. 'Mr. Wouters?' I say. He replies, 'Yes?' My tears well up as I explain to him who I am, Arini, daughter of Rukmini de Witte. Your daughter, Ma.

Hearing that, the man takes me into his arms. There in the doorway, we embrace and cry and don't let go. Mother, I have come home, I am at home with you.

At the end of the day, I walk along the banks of the canal. I know I will come back here someday, because I always come back. The twilight has fallen sideways through the trees, sliding across the roofs of the few cars parked by the side of the road, bouncing off puddles on the sidewalk and the tops of blond heads. Amsterdam. City centre. I walk past groups of tourists and pastry shops that give off the warm aroma of cinnamon. The shops are small and quiet, full of yellow light. I walk past cafes. People sit on frail metal or wood chairs, which are scattered at the front of the cafes under colourful umbrellas. People chat or drink coffee or read a paperback novel or chat and drink coffee. I inhale the bitter, intoxicating aroma of coffee. Going further, I see the lights on the side of the canal turn on, controlled by some mysterious distant force. *Simsalabim*, like magic. We often see this part of the city in films or made into postcards/paintings/photographs. Everything is warm and yellowish, even though the trees are already withered; there's only their wooden fingers scratching the pink-and-purple twilight sky. I am alone, clutching the greenish iron rod of the bridge railing. The surface of the canal ripples a little because there is a wind blowing. It reflects the lights and the shadows of the faces that look into the rippling water. Imperfect reflection. If the wind stops blowing, the water will become still, like glass. But I continue walking, while the sun sinks to the other side of the world. Night falls. Darkness is creeping up from the horizon like watercolours dripping on paper, and before I know it, every inch of the sky has been covered. There are no stars, only a half-moon peering sheepishly through the clouds.

I walk. I wonder where I am now. I read neon-lit signs. Marijuana. Pool tables. Juicebar. Smokey coffee shop. Hash weed skunk white dolphin northern light royal dolphin. Marihuana. Then, suddenly, I'm showered in red light, an artificial blood-red colour, and there I am — the famous Red

Light District of Amsterdam. I find myself staring at the girls behind the window, who don't look back at me because they only stare at the men who walk by. Those girls, how did they get here? They are very young and beautiful. Undressed or half dressed, staring. I cannot stop staring.

But then I think of my daughter and myself and my mother, and there is a lump in my throat, so I quickly leave. The girls behind the windows still do not look at me.

PART TWO

PART TWO

Come, butterfly
It's late —
We've miles to go together.

BASHŌ MATSUO (TRANSLATED BY LUCIEN STRYK)

HANA

The soldier imagined his hands cupping a pair of breasts. The size was average, but the tips were wide, ripe, and pink. He imagined his fingers stroking and pinching so that the nipples hardened like candied red plums on white rice. Then he imagined candied plums. Then he imagined rice, freshly cooked and still hot, these very white and fragrant grains. He imagined eating until he vomited because his stomach could no longer hold the rice, and then he'd make love to a woman so beautiful that she didn't seem real. The woman must be a goddess, a spirit, because every inch of her skin shone like a supernatural being's skin would. An angel.

Sometimes the man cried or howled. He was a mad man, but he was hardly the only one. Once, in the past, at a regular morning assembly, he had witnessed his commander lose his mind and randomly kill someone. The unlucky bastard had been one of their captive American soldiers. In one cry, the man's head had rolled into a muddy puddle, gallons of warm blood spurting into the air from the stump of his neck. Sometimes he, the soldier, had turned away and cried silently when something like that happened. He knew he had hardly been the only one. Sometimes he had laughed out loud. He knew he had not been the only one then, either.

The man imagined his hands in a distant past, when he still had a pair of hands. When he finally woke up, his hands were already gone.

1953.

We switch to another man, to another place and time. This man used to be a photographer, and he always thought of blood when he entered the darkroom to develop photographs. He imagined the womb, he slipped into it to witness the creation of a foetus. Then he became that foetus, curled up and sleeping and hiding, with all that blood enveloping him. How he longs to be in the darkroom again now. That room, this darkroom, hasn't functioned in nearly seven years. He opens the door.

How do you inhale blood? he wonders as his darkroom comes to life. *How do you breathe blood?* His mind wanders. He thinks, *we did it when we were foetuses.* As a foetus, we breathe not air but the oxygen bubbles contained in our mother's blood. Then we are born, and we forget everything — how it was, how it felt. Meanwhile, we can only imagine the blood-red darkness covering us like a heavy blanket.

Here, the man still has everything that he will need. His beloved camera, a high-quality 1943 Kine Exakta, has been taken out from its resting place, even though it's only here to be looked at; to be a token, if you like. He still has a 35mm roll of film that he hasn't touched since he returned from service in Yokohama after the Second World War. The roll has been stored in a special refrigerator for the past six years. Bottles of alcohol. A box of cotton. Running water. Emulsion-coated paper. Trays for the chemicals. These little details feel so familiar, like coming home. A bottle of Ansco acid, cans of hydroquinone, sodium sulfate, and Mallinckrodt carbonate, as well as Kodak potassium bromide, which he mixes with clean water in a standard measure. Clothesline. Clothespins. Etc.

He takes a deep breath. His nose catches a whiff of chemical scent, but he imagines he is actually breathing blood into his lungs.

How do you do this?

In the blink of an eye, he is there again, and he has not forgotten what it feels like.

The former soldier woke up. Morning had not yet arrived, so Hanako, his wife, was still sound asleep beside him, snoring softly, like a pet with a full belly. But the man had forgotten what it felt like to have his belly full. He might have felt it a long time ago, as a child, or in his previous life, but never again. Months had passed. Nobody in that country could tell you what it felt like to be full since the war began, and even after the war was over. You were just trying to survive from day to day, eating whatever appeared in front of you.

The war was over, and the man had returned to his hometown. He opened his eyes. Darkness was enveloping him. His eyes itched, and he raised one hand to rub them before remembering that he no longer had any hands.

He started moaning.

Hanako woke up. *Shh, please calm down*, she whispered.

The darkness was so dense that for a few terrifying moments, he thought he had lost both his eyes as well.

1953.

The dark room is drenched in a blood-red glow that he remembers from his previous life as a United States Navy war photographer. He was only twenty-eight years old when, in the summer of 1945, he landed on the island of Honshu with thousands of other American troops who were preparing to carry out the military occupation of Japan. General Douglas MacArthur was already based in Tokyo, so it was August, of course. A month later the Japanese would officially admit their defeat on board the *U. S. S. Missouri*. The man closes his eyes and reminisces about the wave of heat that hit his face when he arrived on the island. He remembers the smell of something burning. The smell of death, maybe. As it happens, Yokohama and Tokyo had already been burned to the ground by the air strikes. But did the smell really exist? He doesn't want to try to remember.

He moves slowly, wanting to occupy each minute as best as he can.

Someone once asked him what he remembered the most from the battlefield and the long years of documenting the warfare. *I don't remember the colours*, the man had said. *But I do remember the smell.* How strange — death and destruction actually have all the colours we never imagine can exist until we see them with our own eyes, but even in our memory, the colours can fade into black-and-white, just like a photograph produced by a black-and-white film roll. But a smell can never be forgotten.

He remembers replying to that person with a question of his own. *Have you ever smelled a pool of blood?*

The man had yelled at his wife on the first day he had returned home, because what had she known about his suffering? *Have you ever smelled a pool of blood?* he had snapped at her. That night he told her, Hanako, to lie down on the tatami, with her legs opened wide, as wide as possible, so that he could humiliate her, disgrace her, torture her, because the only smell of blood the woman had ever known was her own dirty blood that came out of the hole in her crotch. On that same night, the man discovered that Hanako was menstruating, and he was furious. *You whore. You useless whore.*

How could that man have forgotten how beautiful Hanako had been? She was very beautiful, she shone like a supernatural being. She didn't ask what had happened in the war. She did not ask why he no longer had arms.

Because she had always been a good wife, she bent down on the floor to welcome her husband, who had been away for so long to a place she could never imagine.

Because she had always been a good wife, she then welcomed her husband on the futon, after first removing her work apron, pants, and shirt.

1953.

The first step:

The door, of course, must be closed. You have to make sure that all the gaps are filled so that no light can come in and ruin all your efforts. Light spoils everything when you place your luck on a darkroom. If you are lucky enough, you will gain the beauty of that darkness at the end of the day.

So her name was Hana or Hanako, Hanako or Hana, he muses. Maybe her name was Hanako and then shortened to Hana for convenience, or her name was Hana, but somehow his memory now half-believes that the woman's name was Hanako. He had once looked for the meaning. In Japanese, Hana means flower, while Hanako means flower child. *Nothing makes sense*, he mutters to himself. Nothing makes any sense at all. The war has been over for almost a decade, but he still can't be sure how he feels about the nation, about Japan. Not sane, obviously. Those people are really not sane, but then, who is?

Nonetheless, he still remembers that name.

Unconsciously he starts humming. It is a sad song, a

Japanese song he used to occasionally hear at the naval barracks at night, being sung by some people far away. They sang sad songs at night when they thought no one was listening. In the morning, they would be quiet. They stared but did not point. You wanted to greet them. You wanted to say, *hey, it's alright*. You also wanted to turn back time or, with equal intensity, find someone to blame because the world was such a terrible place. Now you reminisce about the war, with confusion and awe.

The second step:

The 35mm roll is no longer cold. He takes a deep breath to calm himself. With the aid of a scrap of unused film, he slowly rolls up, then pulls out the precious film negative — slowly then quickly, like peeling off dead skin. Now he has to load the film onto the reel to be placed in the tank. He can still do it. All of this is like dance moves well recorded in our joints, right? A muscle memory. Yes, of course. Next, he makes sure that the temperature of the developer mixture has reached sixty-eight degrees Fahrenheit, then he pours the liquid into the film tank. He sets the timer, he comforts himself a little by turning the tank continuously, agitating the film, until the timer rings. He replaces the developer mixture with stop bath, then goes back to doing the same thing with the tank, and then once again with the fixer, after the stop bath. After he is done pouring and shaking, he cleans the negative with running water and a wad of cotton that has been dipped in a little bit of alcohol. Then he dries it. Time passes like nothing. He is in a darkroom. How comfortable. There is a slight chance that the roll has spoiled with age, but it is a risk he has to take.

The third step:

Finally, he brings the negative to the enlarger. He remembers — the emulsion side down. He can still do it. He still can. *Be careful*. He holds his breath as he slides the negatives into place (with the emulsion side down) and returns the carrier to the enlarger.

The fourth step:

The man waited.

Next to him on the futon, Hanako was crying, she was trying hard not to cry, but she was crying. In the dark, he knew that the woman was stuffing a fist into her mouth to muffle the sound of her crying, or maybe to stop her sniffling, who knew. It didn't work. Her tears seeped into the air like rainwater pouring down through the cracks of the leaves of palm trees on the battlefield. On the battlefield, he thought, we never had any shelter from the rain. He stared at the darkness and waited. His nose sniffed blood. His wife's vagina was oozing that smelly and dirty blood of hers. It was only natural to happen every month, but the man still felt an anger rising in his throat at being denied what he wanted.

Do you remember? he wanted to say to her. They had heard the faint sound of the Zero fighter plane; the plane had flown over a patch of sky in the distance, slowly approached them and then, suddenly, sped past them and, even though they were subconsciously waiting for it, the sound of the aircraft engine still made them feel as if their heart had been yanked off its stalk, and that had been it —that had been their first time experiencing such a thing. But it had been a time when all the pain had not yet started. He and Hanako had just stood there gaping, staring at the sky. A meadow. They could see the river flowing quietly from there. The grass had swayed in the breeze. Hanako had worn a *yukata*[9] with flickers of fireflies, grass, and a flowing river, all made of threads; she walked along

9   cotton summer kimono

the meadow in a pair of *geta*.[10] They were heading to a festival in the village square. They still went, in the end. Hours later, night fell, and the village square was lit up with many lanterns. Drumbeats and music and dancing made them forget.

The man remembered what it was like to wait for someone to come, anyone, to save him or kill him. He had fallen into the trench with his crushed arms bleeding incessantly, half of his face immersed in the mud, but he managed to roll over and lie on his back so that his gaze swept across the sky. He remembered waiting to die, or live, as he counted the Zeros and enemy planes flying above him, shaped like tiny birds. The battle was still going on around him, but time had seemed to stop. He had counted, one by one — the number of planes, the sound of bodies falling to the ground, the sound of gunfire, the screams. He remembered that the Zero had another name: A6M.

Do you know, Hanako? he wanted to say to his wife. *Your brother died on a kamikaze mission.* He flew the Yokosuka MXY7, or its other name, Ohka — the cherry blossom.

1953.

His eyes well up with tears. The former photographer straightens himself up, somewhat taken aback, and his teardrop lands safely on his collar instead of on the enlarger board. The tears were brackish at the corners of his mouth, salty like sea water. Doctors have told him that he has shellshock, but then who doesn't? Most of them experience it, those who went to the battlefields to observe, to watch, to capture events and make them eternal. He sighs. Step four: focus. Sometimes it is so easy to do. Sometimes he gives up and falls apart.

He wipes the trace of his tear with his sleeve.

---

10   traditional wooden sandals

The fourth step:

After turning the enlarger on, he sets the f-stop as wide as possible, then adjusts the position of the board and head of the enlarger while setting the focus. His heartbeat speeds up. He closes his eyes. This is the moment. The room is still being bathed in the red glow of the safe light and all he can think of is all the blood he has seen in his life ... his beautiful wife, leaning against two pillows as she spread her legs wide, to give birth to their dead baby girl ... and that poor woman, Hana ... now his heart is jolting so hard, as if it's about to run away, escaping through his throat and jumping out of his mouth. Will his heart stop? Did his friends who died on the battlefield feel the pain when a bullet pierced *their* heart? One time, someone died, and he moved closer to take a picture of the blood flowing from the gaping wounds. He approached, carrying a camera. Many times, someone died.

He waits a moment, then opens his eyes. Now he can see the woman's image on the enlarger board, Hana or Hanako, in black-and-white. This is their first meeting in nearly seven years.

1945. Year Shōwa 20.

The man's wife, Hanako, hurried along with a group of people to the only house in the village that had a radio. They said the Deity would speak through that thing.

People had already gathered when she arrived. Everything was silent except for the box that could create sounds, perched on the surface of a rickety table, and for a moment there was an empty pause, then suddenly, very suddenly, the voice of an unknown man burst through, along with a crackle of static, and instantly every man and woman fell to their knees on the dusty ground, and for Hanako the voice seemed to punch her hard in the chest with an invisible fist and she couldn't breathe, she couldn't, and she couldn't move even an inch closer because her legs suddenly lost all feeling. In all their lives, no one had ever seen the Emperor in person, let alone heard him speak, but there he was, in the midst of them all. *What is he saying?* His speech was soft and tired. He spoke in a song that awakened every hair on Hanako's body; his words were not uttered so fast that they would be hard to catch, but not that slowly either, as if the man, the Deity, didn't want to be suffering for too long. Hanako looked down, slumped on the ground just like everyone else. *The time has come when we must suffer the unsufferable,* the voice told them. The language he used was unusual, foreign, his was the language of heaven. Hanako supported her weight with one hand, and she slowly prostrated on the ground, just as everyone else did. She was trembling. She knew that her husband would now come home because the war was over, even though her brother would never come home because he was dead. Although she didn't cry, everyone else around her was weeping softly and wearily.

1953.

I'm sorry, he mutters to the shadow of the woman. *I'm sorry, please forgive me.* He lets his hands move by themselves, without thinking. Now Hana will be reborn on a sheet of paper through a process of burning. She will be here, and she will accept the man's apology.

The fifth step:

Paper on the enlarger board. This time the f-stop is set in the narrowest aperture. The man grits his teeth and begins to burn the paper with light.

In the morning the woman would say—

Please open your mouth. Slow down, please. Eat up, this is all we have.

They came today. I saw the Americans getting off the warships in the harbour. Many of them. They will settle down for some time. Suddenly they are everywhere. What do you think will happen to us?

Open your mouth again, please.

We'll be fine. I've eaten myself full. Are you full too? Very good. Let's please get up for a moment and go out. The weather is fine right now.

The woman, Hanako, would talk and talk, even if no one felt full and no one would be okay. She would smile and coax while her husband stared through her, a thousand kilometres away. In the afternoon, she would bring hot water that had been boiled on the stove, put it in a wooden bucket, and then place the bucket on the tatami and slowly undress her husband. She would bathe her husband like she would a baby: starting with his feet, which were clean because they didn't step on anything, then the calves, thighs, buttocks, stomach, every inch of his goose-bumped skin, and every part of his shaking body. She worked on him briskly but not harshly. She never asked and never wanted to know. She did not ask where her husband's arms were, even as the wet cloth rubbed against his chest and ribs and moved up to the stumps of his arms. She would only pause for a moment as if she were stunned by them anew, then she would resume her work. The wounds had dried up a long time ago and were now tinged white. But Hanako still didn't ask.

At night she would say nothing as she watched her husband's penis become rigid and hard and stand upright in front of her, because she knew what was going to happen. Her husband would fall apart, and Hanako would endure everything without saying anything.

1953.

The sixth step:

The developer activates light-sensitive crystals on the paper, so that any part of the paper that has been exposed to the light from the enlarger will turn dark. The former photographer blinks, and Hana, or Hanako, appears before him on paper inside a plastic tray filled with developer. He thinks of the million light-sensitive crystals that now form the dark patches of Hana's black hair, peeking out from under her headcover. Women wore headcovers as they worked all day on the fields to grow anything edible, and the man remembers the day he first saw Hana passing by on her way to somewhere, wearing that headcover, strands of hair dangling into her eyes. Her eyes were very dark. The man is daydreaming — he's been daydreaming a lot lately. He shakes the plastic tray that contains the developer solution and the photograph until the timer goes off again. Then the clean water. Then the tray of stop bath, so that the chemicals in the developer stop reacting. The plastic trays are lined up in the usual order. This is after this, and this after this. Clean water, then more clean water. He is waiting.

Fixer solution: its job is to remove unexposed crystals in the emulsion so that later our photo can be safely exposed to normal light without changing colour. Like memories do, it removes the sad parts that we don't want.

This time his wife's genitalia were clean and bloodless. If only he still had a pair of hands, wouldn't the man be able to do whatever he wanted? He wanted to reach down for the warm hole he had always liked, he wanted to touch it and caress it, and while doing so, he would observe Hanako's face and watch the sweat oozing from her hairline. The woman would not make a sound, but her mouth would be open. *Why are you still with me?* he asked. *I can no longer touch you.* But what the hell did he care. Sometimes the scars throbbed, and Hanako didn't know that her husband could no longer feel anything in his chest and stomach. Maybe the nerves were dead, maybe not. Either way, he felt dead.

That night the man learned to fuck his wife without arms. His memories moved back and forth, flashing; these various memories seemed to overlap but also sat side by side. He was back to being a little boy who was just learning to walk. He saw the white hand of a woman holding his; it belonged to his mother, who was long dead, and it was the hand that had been ready to catch him when he fell. He remembered falling so many times — on the tatami, on a wooden floor, on a dirt road that was wet and damp from the rain, on his mother's lap. He remembered that his mother had a very tiny blunt nose. Then he remembered the day they had raided a village in Guam, in the Mariana Islands, and raped every woman they could find there.

His wife, Hanako, grimaced in pain but the man didn't stop. He wanted to be on top of her even though he had to fall repeatedly because he no longer had arms to support himself. And in that village, in his previous life, he remembered a woman who had screamed and pleaded to him in a foreign language, perhaps for him to stop, but he hadn't stopped. He never knew the woman's name. He only remembered the sweet and fishy taste of her body. His mother had said, *Come on, walk to that table. Then come back here.* Come back. The man had held the unnamed woman's hands behind her back so that he could strike her from behind. Around him, Watanabe and Yamada had been doing the same thing to two other women. His mother had said, *Come back to me.* His wife grimaced in pain.

He had sex with the two women at the same time, as if reality and memory were solid substances that could be woven together and fused into one. As if he was being possessed, he thrust again and again, and he thought to himself: *All women taste the same.* His wife was an extraordinarily beautiful woman, and the screaming woman had been anything but beautiful, yet they felt the same. Now he shut down all his five senses, and for a moment he was nowhere except in the bodies of the two women. Then another day they had stormed another village. There he had chosen a girl who had been so young that he had hesitated for a moment, but it had not been enough to stop him. The girl had seemed to break under the weight of his big, strong body. Maybe she had died. There might have been one very brief second when the man had wondered if the young girl did indeed die, but when he was done, he didn't look back at the small body he had left behind.

The girl had tasted just the same. Then his mother said, *Come back to me.* Now he was back. He had come home.

1953.

The former photographer imagines telling his wife about a woman he once fell in love with. A Japanese woman, he would say. She lived in a village in Yokohama; we could see the harbour from there. It was the harbour where we had landed. Our occupation of Japan only ended a year ago, but this was a long time before I returned home, before I returned to you.

That woman was married to a former Imperial soldier who was permanently disabled after a bomb had exploded near him. His last name was Onda. Onda-san, that's all I know. That woman's name, my dear, was Hana or Hanako. If her name was Hana then it means flower, if it was Hanako then it means flower child. I don't know which one. So the man was half-crazy when he returned from the battlefield. He had lost both his arms. Not important. On the battlefield we will always lose something; a pair of arms is nothing. But he became half-crazy.

I fell in love with that woman, his wife.

The former photographer imagines telling his wife about a sin he knows will never be forgiven. He will tell her today, he thinks; whatever is going to happen will happen. Meanwhile, after each photo has been processed in fixer solution and has been washed under running water for ten minutes, the man hangs it on the clothesline to dry.

In the first photo, Hana appears to be emitting light.

Five months had passed since her husband had come home, and today, she mused, Hanako would tell him. Or not. Should she tell him? She woke up very early, long before even the chickens, birds, rabbits, dogs, cats, and small insects woke up. She believed that no other human was awake, but then she found her husband lying with his eyes open, staring at the ceiling of the house. 'Hanako,' he said simply, as if the name was written on the ceiling, and he was merely reading it out loud. Hanako was startled, even though she didn't show it. So, instead, she slowly got up. She smiled. She didn't know if her husband saw her smile, but she smiled. She stood up on her two feet, folded her futon, and stashed it in a neat pile in the wardrobe. For a moment she glanced at the man lying on the futon, her husband, who at the same time was also a stranger; he lay there just like he always did, in the daytime and all the time, that stranger. Then Hanako turned away. All the weariness and despair that had been overcoming her seconds ago had passed. She left the room. Her husband didn't ask where she was going.

In fact, she didn't know where she was going or what to do. She stepped out of the house and greeted the cold early dawn. There were still a few hours before the sun rose. She looked up and saw the stars, thousands of stars twinkling in the perfect black sky; she counted the stars one by one and thought about the tales of Heike and Genji that her grandmother used to tell her when she was a child. Her grandmother had been a peasant from Shodoshima. On certain nights, she would take Hanako out of the house and then point at the sky while sighing, 'Awaine Boshi — the millet and rice stars.' You search the sky in autumn to see if the millet and rice stars have moved across the sky. When they occupy a certain angle, you know to harvest rice and then plant millet, and vice versa in late spring, when to harvest millet and then plant rice. Hanako used to be a child who had believed with all her heart that Heike and Genji were still fighting each other in the night sky after thousands of years. Even now, she was looking up and wondering when their war would end.

The mortal's war on earth had ended. Hanako continued her steps. She muttered to herself, *step carefully*. She thought of her husband, who had returned from the battlefield as someone else. This someone else slept by her side every night and woke up by her side every morning. This someone else made love to her every night and sometimes in the morning if he wanted to. Hanako didn't know if she was running away from that someone else.

From the height of the hill in the village, she could see that the harbour and the American warships were sound asleep. She could see the moonlight reflecting off the seawater into an illusion of a field of diamonds. Not far from there, she saw the city of Yokohama, or what was left of it. Debris. Traces of the dead. *Step carefully, Hanako*, she told herself. Someone heard her murmuring. And she saw the man, who was looking straight at her.

1946. January. I'm not going to lie, sometimes I did follow her all day without her knowing it. But I'm not lying if I tell you that that early dawn, we accidentally met each other under a Japanese cypress tree that they called *hinoki*. Cypresses grew everywhere in Yokohama, and in that village. I liked them: I loved their scent and the feeling of being protected when I sat under them. Hana saw me and I saw her. She moved backwards. I said, It's okay, but she didn't understand me.

Why did I fall in love with her? I do not know. There was no reason that could make sense. Maybe I saw the suffering in her. I was trained for that after all, seeing the suffering in everything. Maybe I just simply *saw* her. I was suffering, too.

At that time, I was writing a letter to you, my dear, under that hinoki tree, with the help of a lantern that I'd brought from the barracks. I was telling you how that week I'd been sent to Hiroshima and Nagasaki (oddly enough, it turned out that the two cities were located very far from Yokohama), where nothing remained but rubble and traces of the dead. I had to take pictures of all of that. I was suffering too, and Hana saw it in me.

The man said something. What did it mean?

Hanako moved back two more steps. 'Forgive me,' she said, bowing several times. 'Forgive me.' In town she had run into American soldiers many times, but not like this, and certainly not at half past three in the morning when the rest of the world was asleep. Hanako realised that they were alone. The man stared at her without blinking. *Stop looking at me like that.*

She turned away. She felt the American man's gaze fixed on her back. When she thought that the man had stopped staring, Hanako turned her head to steal a glance, but the man had not yet looked away. He was still staring. He sat at the root of a hinoki tree with its leaves half-gone, writing a letter with the help of a lantern. Perhaps he was writing to a family member or a lover, someone who was waiting for him to come home.

Hanako walked away thinking, *I was once waiting, too.*

1953.

His watch shows exactly fifteen minutes before noon. The former photographer is still working on processing the second, third, and fourth photos. In these photos Hana takes turns to look peaceful, sad, and confused. Anyone would think that the woman's two feet weren't standing anywhere and that she was just waiting to fall. In the photo she appears to be on a gravel path, then at the edge of a puddle. Then she is in the city, in a ration distribution queue with dozens of other women. Hungry eyes. Weak, thin, tired bodies. Mouths uttering Japanese words, which the man understood to mean *sugar rice a small bottle of soy sauce very small grains of rice sugar and rice*, their lives depending on a small bag of bad rice whose grains were very small; those bags of rice were really very small.

So Hanako returned home, where she thought of a bag of good-quality rice that she'd purposely kept for months, to be cooked when there was something to celebrate. She had used half of it when her husband had returned from the battlefield. Now she intended to use the remaining half. She kept it in a special clay container, high on top of the cupboard, together with her most valuable possession: a silk kimono that she had inherited from her mother, the only item she had brought from home when she had gone to marry her husband. She took the bag of rice from the container; she opened it and poured the contents into a bowl to be washed. Then she washed the rice diligently, careful not to drop a single grain down the drain, for this was all they had. But today she and her husband would eat more luxuriously than usual.

Hanako walked back and forth around the kitchen. She worked on the stove, sweeping away any remaining soot; she boiled water, chopping turnips for a side dish, waiting for the water to boil, putting chunks of radish into boiling water. She waited for the sun to rise. She was waiting for someone to wake up, maybe a neighbour or two; she was waiting for Nakano-san to gallop past their house, groaning, calling for her son who would never come home because he had died in the war. Hanako let her mind wander. Her husband, the stranger, would later say, *You know what I've been through all this time?* Meanwhile she had to hold her tongue so as not to talk back: how would she know about what had happened to someone she didn't even know. (What if Nakano-san's son hadn't died in Manchuria? Would he also have come back as a stranger?) Hanako drained the cooked turnip. Now she had to prepare hot water for bathing her husband.

She made up her mind. Today she would tell her husband, that stranger, that they were expecting a baby.

His beautiful wife, and all the blood that soaked her. The beaming safe light. He is drowning in red light, the colour of red, blood red, and he swims in it. One morning, while emerging from behind the bathroom door, his beautiful wife said that she was pregnant. He still remembers that day, as clear as the thick smell of iron in the blood that hit his nose and made acid rise from his stomach into his throat. Even though the man believed he was used to blood, it was apparently not true; he would never get used to it. The red light still surrounds him. The darkroom is the uterus. This is where creation takes place.

They created that baby. She was not yet two months old, the doctor said, so she resembled a bead lodged in his wife's womb, she was made of blood and breath and (they say) love. It was true that they had been making love every day after the man returned from service in Japan. It was true that they were both relieved to be back together in their tiny house. New Orleans looked the same as when the man had left it for his first assignment to cover the situation at Pearl Harbor, immediately after the Japanese struck, twelve years ago. So after everything was over, he returned to the house, where nothing had really changed, except that now there would be the three of them instead of two. Then the man decided to hang up the camera for good.

They prepared everything. A room overlooking the garden, stripped of all its useless attributes, was cleaned and repainted to prepare for the baby's impending arrival. They shopped. Baby crib, stroller, books about babies, books about baby names. His wife wanted the name Amos (if a boy) or Ava (if a girl). She wanted a room full of stuffed animals. Three months then four months, and his wife's stomach was getting bigger, but the man was getting worse. He never said why.

'Is it a boy?'
    'How would we know.'

'Hopefully it is a boy.'

He stared at the ceiling of the house.

'Why don't you get up from that futon?'

'Don't want to.'

'*Son.*'

The man did not answer. His father was old. The war had added a lot of new wrinkles to his skin — now he was all-hollow and all-empty, as if maggots had eaten him alive without him realising it. Even so, his eyes were still sparkling. 'I'm proud of you,' he kept saying. Of course he was proud; his only son had become a war hero. But that status was useless now.

Hanako brought hot tea on a tray. Her stomach preceded her. It had a baby in it, perhaps a thin and malnourished baby. The man did not have a hunch whether the baby was a boy or a girl. 'Thank you for visiting us, father,' Hanako said. Her father-in-law nodded briefly. He drank the tea. Then he told them about his two daughters who lived with their husbands in Kawasaki, about the situation that was slowly getting better, about harvesting fruit, about his hobby of making handicrafts out of scrap wood from ruined buildings. 'We will be fine,' he said. 'The Americans will not be here forever. They are not terribly bad, although they are completely untrustworthy. They go around handing out sweets and chocolates. American brands. How long haven't you been out of the house? The only thing the next generation will remember of the Americans will be the sweets and chocolates, but other than that, we are alright.'

When his father had left, the man heaved and managed to sit up straight. His wife looked at him but said nothing. 'Bring me a bowl and chopsticks,' said the man. His wife did what he asked. The bowl did not contain rice or miso soup. Hanako said, 'I can always feed you,' but the man ignored her, only slowly moving the toes of his right foot to pinch the two bamboo chopsticks, which were so yellowed and dirty that he wondered why they still had them.

He tried again and again, without success, and the pair of chopsticks continued to slide onto the floor and roll away from him.

Year 20 Shōwa.

That night in March, the sky looked so clean and calm that we could clearly see the stars forming a sky river that flowed to a secret place in heaven. Hanako thought of her husband in some secret place, dead or alive, but he wasn't thinking of her. During this time, he only sent her a few letters, which she kept in the cupboard until finally Hanako received nothing else. *My wife*, that was how her husband began his letters. She read them a few times, then her husband's words became too painful because they were separated by a distance that could not be crossed. So it was March. The American planes came again. The dates were 9 and 10, and in the beginning, the sky was very clean and quiet.

Since January, she had woken up many times in the middle of the night to the sound of sirens howling, announcing air raids. Then it was always the same: she gasped, convulsed, remembering that she was alone, hurriedly looking for outer clothes. The air was so cold, biting cold, *run, run*; she joined Nakano-san and the Kurakawa family to take refuge in their bunker. The earth was shaking. Underground, they were crowded together and shivering with cold. Sometimes Hanako felt a pang of hunger. Sometimes she just couldn't care. Sometimes Kurakawa-san's sickly daughter lost consciousness and collapsed in Hanako's lap. She would hug her the whole night until the girl woke up and asked what was going on or if it was over.

But that night in March, she witnessed the once ink-black and calm sky quickly turning red: as red as fresh, bright blood dripping out of an open wound. The American bomber planes soared high above her head. Fragments of shrapnel and bombs and sharp objects were flying, darting, scattered everywhere. A large fire followed and an intense, burning heat, which felt as if it peeled people's faces from their skulls. After the 9th and 10th had passed, Hanako would hear that over a hundred thousand people died in Tokyo alone. Later, Kobe was destroyed, Toyama was turned into ruins, and by May, not just her area, but half of Yokohama had become ashes. *Do you know, husband?* she wanted to say. *We were running for our lives in such a scurry, trying our best not to get killed.*

That night in March, when they once again took shelter underground and a shower of gravel and dust poured into their lungs with every breath they took, Hanako was still thinking about her husband. She wondered if the man was alive or dead, if he was wounded.

1952.

September. The baby would be born in October, but in early September the former photographer suddenly woke in the middle of the night to the sound of his wife moaning. He gasped and sat up straight. His wife lay covered in sweat, her face completely white. Their mattress was soaked with blood.

He didn't stop to think. He grabbed the car keys, scooped up his wife (*Oh my God, oh my God*, the woman cried); he carried her to the garage and put her into the car and in a flash, he was driving frantically towards the Marine Hospital on State Street.

God only knows how he was able to drive through all those roads without hitting stray dogs or lampposts, mailboxes or rubbish bins or other cars or people who weren't so lucky that they were still on their way home. He sped up as he passed Annunciation Street. The hospital building was visible in front of him, sandwiched in between Leake Road, Henry Clay Avenue, State, and Tchoupitoulas Street. His wife was already half-unconscious. The former photographer stopped at the entrance to the hospital and left his car there with the engine running while he roared for help, *anyone, help us*. A male nurse snatched his wife from his hands, and the former photographer stood there silently for a few moments, examining the fact that he was holding nothing. *We have to get the baby out*, someone said. The former photographer's leg muscles moved, following the sounds. He walked through the corridors lit with beaming white fluorescent lights. There were people wearing white clothes. The delivery room. He wasn't allowed to enter, then he was. The doctor said to someone who was not him, *But there's no heartbeat ...*

Time elapsed. The former photographer realised that there was a large spot of blood on his pyjama top, shaped like an island. Like at a theatre show, or a circus, or a Hollywood silent film, the man watched the surgeons get into their positions, ducking over his wife. Her legs were wide apart. You could see the top of a baby's head, but the baby was dead.

He found his wife's hand. He held it. He felt a weak pulse and then began to count silently.

It was a baby girl. They named her Ava, then brought her home before her burial.

Ava felt cold in my arms. Her eyes were closed and her skin was blue. We dressed her in a doll version of a white lacy communion dress, and we put some blush on her, but her face was still blue. We'd imagined that one day this little girl would be a violinist or a singer, a great actress, a performer, a mathematician. We couldn't let the dreams die, so we buried every detail in the coffin with our daughter. Our dreams. The day before the funeral, the two of us lay on the bed, flanking her in the middle. I had my own dreams for her, but in the end we agreed on every great thing she could achieve when she grew up. For a while, we forgot that our daughter had died; she was just deeply asleep, there between the two of us.

In his dreams the man would fall asleep and then wake up, and sometimes he would say, *Forgive me.* Who knew to whom. He still didn't have arms. Who knew when the nightmare would end. Hanako was haunted by nightmares of her own. Once again, she witnessed her brother saying goodbye before going to join the war, and she and several family members saw him off at the door. They wore pure-white clothes; they were waving a flag. *May the gods keep you safe, may the gods bring you home safely. May Japan win the war.* In her dreams, Hanako again received the official letter from the country that informed her that her older brother had died on a noble mission to defend the Emperor. (*Suicide mission*, she thought, but she kept those thoughts well to herself.) Then, again, she saw her husband off at the door, wearing the same pure-white clothes, waving the same flag, saying the same prayers. The dreams didn't end. But that was alright, they were alright.

Sometimes her husband cried a lot of tears. They were awake many nights. Hanako was reminded of the stories of the undead who staggered through the hell of ash and charcoal, hours after the atomic bombs were dropped on Nagasaki and Hiroshima. Her husband had not experienced that, but he still woke up and cried. They stayed up night after night without end. During the day, Hanako heard the stories about what had happened two years earlier in Saipan: mothers jumping off cliffs while hugging their babies because the American soldiers had arrived to get them. Then, when night fell again, Hanako lay down on her futon and let her tears fall. She thought of these women and their babies as bodies scattered at the bottom of the cliff. She thought of herself. She was going to be a mother, but the stranger next to her didn't care.

Her stomach was already very large, where a creature resided, a creature that was constantly moving in its own strange world. Sometimes, at four in the afternoon, or when she felt really tired after working in the fields, Hanako came back home to rest. She made herself weak tea and went into the bedroom and found her husband still lying there. Hanako lay down beside the man, hearing him breathe, imagining her baby breathing in her belly. How did a foetus breathe? Oh, it breathed blood. The foetus spun, kicked, hiccuped. Every time it kicked, Hanako would put one hand on her stomach to take the kick. She wanted her husband to feel it, but he didn't have hands. He didn't even wake up. He was just delirious, cursing, crying. A year had passed since the war had ended.

The man looks at the eleventh image that slowly materialises in a pool of chemical liquid. There is only a view of the Yokohama landscape in the afternoon, filling the entire photo. He remembers that he'd taken the photo while drunk on sake. It was the weekend, and he and his Navy colleagues had visited a drinking house full of half-naked Japanese women — their breasts the size of saucers poking out of cheap kimonos, ready to be sucked and licked. The men were bored and needed entertainment. American soldiers went there to suck and lick the breasts of half-naked Japanese women.

Then he is back in 1953, to the present and the now. The darkroom is not soundproofed, so he can still hear the sounds his wife is making out there. His wife has called him, but the man chose not to answer. At the end of 1946, the man came home from a drinking house with three or four friends who were singing loudly, then he chose to go his separate way. *Where are you going?* they asked. He shrugged. Thompson the stutterer was singing Frank Sinatra, Tommy Dorsey, 'I'll Never Smile Again'. *Just leave him be*, people said. He left, while his friends continued to sing and exchange heroic stories about the war. Hmm, what good *would* it do? He thinks back to the time when Hana was pregnant. That was great. Back then he didn't think about his wife back at home, hundreds of miles away in New Orleans, United States.

We buried Ava, then everything seemed to be engulfed in pitch darkness. We freefell into a bottomless abyss. You cried and so did I. We cried for months. Grief constantly changed its shape, like water taking the shape of the cup in which it dwells, and suddenly our pet dog was grief, so were your favourite mini cacti, so was a cigarette of mine that twinkled, dying in the evening, so was your Sunday dress, so were you, so was I. Grief was transformed into everything we had loved. My baby left her mark in my arms, it was still cold, I could still hear the sound of soft cloth rubbing against cold skin that she had left behind. We knew she had died, because she was so heavy and cold.

Back to a more distant past: the man bent over the bush to vomit sake mixed with half of the contents of his stomach. He had drunk too much. His head was spinning. He was holding on to a plant or electric pole or a tree, he didn't know. He felt the weight of the camera hanging from his neck like a baby monkey. Isn't that ridiculous? He almost never removed that thing from around his neck, that ridiculous Kine Exakta. He was naked without it. Several Japanese people walked past him, staring in fear. It was twilight. He was standing before an empty field that opened up to an immense orange sky. He was so touched by the beauty in front of him that he once again lifted his ridiculous Kine to his face to snap a picture. In 1953, the camera is perched over there, staring at him quietly and calmly, not blaming, not judging, just sitting there in a corner of the table. Only the Japanese looked at him in fear. What do you see, hey?

Something else had also died between us. At first I didn't realise it, then I realised that our relationship could no longer be repaired. The grief caused it. Also my sins. We come home from the battlefield carrying sins, even though the war is over in the place from which I returned to you. Someone told me that you cheated once or twice when I wasn't around, but I won't blame you.

Disgusting, he thought. The man rubbed the vomit off his mouth. He broke down drunk, and insane. He hated everything. In the drinking house he had been sucking and licking a half-naked Japanese woman's breasts. Both breasts, the left and the right, and the woman sighed and then the man slipped a bank note into her cleavage. But the man knew that what he wanted was another Japanese woman. Now his ears were filled with the remnants of the shrill laughter of the Japanese women in the drinking house. He didn't know what to do because everything was wrong — there wasn't any truth in this world. He was wandering and bobbing, as if that day were his first day in the unit and their ship had suddenly hit a big storm in the middle of the sea. Or as if he were in the battlefield, where he had to aim at a moving object from the shaking deck of a ship — the object a fighter plane that was shot and then plummeted into the sea, taking with it its enemies or its friends. In his mind, that act of falling was always in slow motion.

You fell in love with your former piano teacher. I was fine with it, as he was a good man. I wondered why you decided in the end to stay with me. Everything had been fine for a while. Then Ava died. We stopped being fine.

He found Hana after searching like crazy for some time. The woman was crossing the bridge that divided the Nakamura River in Naka District, carrying a cloth bag containing an old kimono that she had not managed to sell to a used-goods reseller. She was very thin, her body large in only one part. She stared blankly at the road in front of her. The man followed her from afar. They were twenty metres apart, so that Hana wouldn't notice; she was thinking of another crazy man, who never recovered from the war, looming in the dark. The sun slipped behind the horizon in the background and for a moment Hana appeared as a dark, melting silhouette. It was beautiful, deeply touching. The man followed her, stumbling around. He knew where she was but never came too close. He knew where the woman lived with her crazy husband.

In 1953, the man again hears his wife's voice, calling him. At the end of 1946, he did not hear a sound except for the sound of the steps that Hana created — *clack-clack-clack* along the bridge, and then on gravel. His own steps made no sound because he was always adept at tiptoeing and hiding. The man was an experienced natural hunter.

I will tell you about my sins. You already know most of them. This is the worst.

The man grabs the pincers. He nimbly saves the paper from drowning in the fixer liquid because the timer has now gone off, because he doesn't want anything to drown anywhere anymore. At the end of 1946, Hana was picturing herself drowning in the Nakamura River while, expertly, the man was following her far behind, so drunk that he felt he was drowning in the fresh, breathable air. Time elapsed. The day turned into night. The lights began burning in every house because the Japanese were no longer afraid to turn them on, because there were no more air raids, no more enemy jetfighters that might be attracted by house lights that went on at night. In 1953, this time and now, he hangs that last photograph on a stretch of rope next to all the versions of Hana that stare, say something, say nothing, bend forward, move about, stay in place. It is over. There is nothing left.

Year 21 Shōwa.

That American man again. From the corner of her eye, Hanako caught sight of the man moving like a shadow in the distance. For a moment, she hesitated, but it was him, the same man she had seen, sitting under a hinoki tree. She tried not to think. Her body was heavy, the baby turning inside her, perhaps curling up and dreaming. Then the baby woke up when it felt that she, Hanako, was scared. *Hush.* The baby kicked once. *Do not look back.* She accelerated her pace. *Do not be afraid.* Night fell

the Japanese were no longer prohibited by the government from lighting their houses, nor did they need to hide in the dark anymore. Every time night fell, I was mesmerised by the artificial lights that were born one after another, enveloping the surface of the hill. How touching, because we know the meaning, that lights in houses symbolise a time of peace. Even so, there was no peace in me. I followed that woman as I often did. I'm telling you, I was usually just immortalising the woman in a roll of film that belonged to me personally, that I didn't submit to the Navy archives. But at that moment, I wanted her body

she shivered. Hanako realised that the man knew she knew. So she decided to turn into a dark alley flanked by two houses, hoping that the road would lead to somewhere. If the road led nowhere, she thought she would just hide there. She moved quickly but carefully. *Calm down, calm down*, she whispered to herself. The baby was not calm, it was kicking

I saw her turn into a dark alley flanked by two houses where she was immediately engulfed by the darkness. What was I thinking at that time? I have no idea. Most of me feared for her safety. What if the darkness swallowed her alive and she never came out again? The other part of me still wanted her body, then my own body reacted, tensing and hardening beyond my control. Delicious and painful. I remember how my breath began to rush. I sped up. Now I was chasing her

Stop it, she begged. Hanako ran through the dark alley in front of her, begging her baby to stop kicking. Sweat started to pour. Far ahead, she saw a glimmer of light. Hanako didn't know where she was — maybe in another district, maybe nowhere. There was no one. No sound. She considered turning around, then remembered that the man was behind her. Where to, now? She begged the gods to show her the right direction, but there was no answer.

When we brought Ava home from the hospital, we wrapped her in a soft blanket given by a kind nurse. You held her in the car all the way. You held her close to your chest. I did not tell you that the bundle containing the body of our baby reminded me of the bundle that the Japanese woman had carried at that time. It contained a very beautiful kimono, but its beauty wasn't enough for the used-goods reseller. As I cornered the woman on an empty street, her bundle fell to the ground, and I caught a glimpse of sky-blue fabric embroidered with silvery threads — a patch of sky and little silver birds flying. Your bundle contained our baby.

Hanako found herself on an empty street she had never

been on before. Most of the buildings there had been destroyed during air raids and abandoned by their owners: residential houses, grocery stores, a small shrine with a statue of the god of wisdom, Omoikane, damaged almost beyond recognition. Where to, now? She was about to run, but it was too late. The American man emerged from the darkness like a demon.

I am a devil. I'm not the man you should accept back by your side.

Their eyes met. Hanako dropped the cloth bag containing her mother's kimono, which she had tried to sell that afternoon without success. The American man didn't look like a devil now, but his eyes were red, his whole face was red, his body was drenched in sweat from running, and he smelled like stale sticky rice. He said something. American language. Hanako said, *No, please.* She wanted to run, she *had* to run, but her body wouldn't move. Why could she always run when the sirens went off but not now?

Please, I told her, because I have suffered so much and want to come home and want to come home and want to come home. I never wanted this. I joined the Navy because my father wanted me to be of use, but I only knew how to shoot with a camera. Flowers, butterflies, smiling people. Not endless war or blood or death. Not this either. Even so, my dear wife, that night I caught Hana and held her hands behind her back so that she couldn't run anywhere. She started screaming but no one, no one heard her but me. I tightened my grip. I forced her to lie down on the ground while holding each hand at the side of her beautiful head. The skin of her wrists was brittle like paper and rough from the weather, and I saw that my grip left white and pink finger marks.

Hanako struggled uselessly, then realised that the American man was looking at her from above with tears in his eyes. The man's tears fell onto Hanako's face while he lowered his pants and began to rape her. Hanako closed her eyes tightly so that she could no longer see the darkness but only the stars inside her head, forming a sky river ...

Her belly was so big between us. I thought, poor thing, that unborn baby.

The American was still crying when he finished with her a moment later.

1953.

He comes out of the darkroom. His wife is waiting for him. 'Hello,' she says. 'Hello,' the man answers. 'You were in there a long time,' his wife says. The man nods then says, 'Just like before.' He sees that his wife is standing very erect, tall and imposing, and she wears neat travelling clothes and gloves and a hat. A suitcase is on the floor at her feet. His wife says that she will never come back. The man nods. He knows. He counts the number of buttons on his wife's jacket, then analyses the beige colour of the blouse. Is this beige the colour of skin or of egg? He says nothing and feels nothing. Are they going to separate temporarily or divorce? Is the red of her hat the same colour as blood or carnation petals? She looks beautiful and gentle. The man says, *Goodbye.* His wife replies by saying that she is taking with her a portrait of her that the man had taken, long before they married. *You made me look too pretty in that photo. Thank you. Goodbye. Thank you.*

I left, running away crazily. I left the woman lying on the dirty ground with her legs wide open. I imagined that one of the woman's legs then fell limply to the side. Maybe she was moaning because of the pain I caused. Maybe she didn't cry. She would be more worried about her belly and worried that the pain she was feeling was caused by her baby. The next day

I sent a formal letter requesting my discharge from the Navy, while on that very day, as soon as I left, Hana found the baby was pushing to get out. How do I know? I don't know, really.

But this is what crossed my mind: the woman, lying on the dirty ground, blinked to get the sweat out of her eyes, then she rose to her feet with difficulty. She was someone who always found her feet, unlike me or the other troubled man she lived with. She stood up and walked, in pain, looking for her way home even though it meant going back through the dark passage. She carried the kimono she inherited from her mother. She thought of her mother. She thought of me. She thought of me without cursing me or forgiving me.

She headed home. Amniotic fluid mixed with blood poured out between her legs. She walked very far until she found a small clinic that she had visited once with a neighbour. The place was closed, but someone was about to open the door for her — perhaps an exhausted old doctor, maybe a young, energetic nurse leaving from a day's work. I'm sure someone opened the door.

Now I stand in my own doorway and watch the woman I love more than anything leave me. Then, like in a dream, I return to the darkroom, which I occupy just as I used to inhabit my mother's womb. I close the door. Hana was waiting in front of the clinic, and someone opened the door for her. I stare at photos of mine hanging by the clothespins. Hana looked down between her thighs and found the baby's head sticking out. Now I look at her, Hana, which in Japanese means flower.

I'm sorry, I say, and she will forgive me. She has forgiven the world, the war, the world war, and she forgives the men who caused her so much suffering. As she lay in a patient bed, possibly the only one that was available in that small clinic, she would give birth to a baby boy or girl, and she would stop struggling against the destruction that had already occurred. She looked forward and saw hope. They all stood up to greet the beginning of a new dawn.

For her, the baby was hope. She would return home with another bundle containing her precious little baby. The baby was crying, so she cried too, but this time for joy and relief. Her mad husband would now sit up to greet her. Maybe for a moment he wouldn't be insane. Maybe now her husband would remember to say *okaeri*[11] after Hana shouted *tadaima*.[12] I love imagining all that. To me, the man was nameless and faceless, but I could imagine the corners of his lips lifting into a lopsided smile. He recognised the baby. Even though he no longer had the arms to carry the baby, he would find his own way.

Hana or Hanako. I look at her portraits one more time before finally leaving for good, leaving my darkroom, the womb, so that I can be reborn into the real world in the present and the now. I remember to close the door.

11 Japanese: welcome home
12 Japanese: I am home

I know. I was there. I saw the great void in your soul, and you saw mine.

SEBASTIAN FAULKS, *BIRDSONG*

AYAKA

These days, Dara always buys the same snack from a tiny mini-mini-convenience store, one that is squeezed between a post box and some kind of gate at the entrance of a strange two-story parking garage. These days she strolls around every morning and evening, then buys snacks when she gets hungry. The snack is always the same — an *onigiri*, or Japanese rice ball — but the filling varies every day, because it feels like an adventure. Some are filled with candied plums, tuna mayonnaise, salmon chunks, shredded *bonito*, or fish eggs. Some contain vegetables. Some contain rice that has been mixed with all kinds of things.

These days, Dara sometimes sees a certain Japanese woman wandering around, like herself. She is very beautiful, a shining angel. She has a paralysing beauty. Sometimes they, the two women, cross paths at that tiny mini-mini-market, but the Japanese woman doesn't buy anything, she just hangs around in front of the buzzing, dewy refrigerator. Maybe she likes to try and figure out which of those sugary drinks wouldn't be too fattening, but then decides to leave instead. Dara once saw that the woman's fingernails were short and decorated with imitation crystals the colour of cherries. Every now and then, an index finger floated to the glass door of the refrigerator, stayed there for a few seconds, then left a wet trail that pooled and dripped. Dara wondered if maybe the woman was not Japanese, but a tourist who got lost every day while trying to navigate the city, a tourist who was somehow already familiar with this special mini-mini-market. But then winter rolled into summer. In winter, Dara likes to go in there because she enjoys the warm gust of wind from the heating above her head. She would wander around wearing two, three layers of clothing, as well as stiff new boots that leave oozing scabs in between her toes. Meanwhile, the Japanese woman would, as usual, look effortlessly beautiful, her fur hat only slightly wind-blown, so that it perched, gently tilted, on her head. In summer, Dara is tempted by the dew that runs down the glass door of the refrigerator. Dara has seen this woman in multiple seasons, so it seems that she is, in fact, not a tourist, but probably a local. Should Dara say, 'Hello, hello, how are you?' *Sumimasen, nihongo wakarimasen.* (*Sorry, I don't understand Japanese.*) In summer, the woman would wear a wide woven hat. Dara would wander around, her sandals expensive but hand-me-down Birkenstocks (from a cousin of hers in Jakarta, given to her several years ago); she'd wear a light polka-dotted dress that would cling to a large patch of sweat on her back. Then they would both leave, but first, Dara would pay for the onigiri she had chosen. This one would be sprinkled with sesame seeds.

She will not choose any other kind of snack.

Every night, after wandering and getting lost many times, because she is not good at reading maps or following the instructions of the female robot voice of the Google Maps app, she will cook quite a bit of dinner for herself and her husband. She is good at following easy online recipes. Her schedule is as follows: cooking every other day, eating out every weekend when she is too lazy to cook and her husband has just received his pay. They sit together every night and eat, exactly at eight o'clock, after her husband has come home from work. He always sits with his back towards the floor-to-ceiling window that displays the glowing top of the Umeda Sky building in the distance. Her husband always asks her, just to fill the silence: 'What did you do today?'

Dara stares at the glowing Umeda Sky and then at her husband. He is a very different man from the previous one, Dara's ex-boyfriend, who left her shortly before they were supposed to get married, because he loved another woman. Her husband doesn't smoke, for one thing, and he is neat and tidy, a good-kid type who doesn't want to disappoint his strict, wealthy Sumatran parents (his family comes from Palembang). He has a flat personality and tends to be boring; he is predictable, like the eternally rainy weather in Jakarta. Also predictably, as a fan of Japanese anime and manga with parents who could afford most things that he wanted, he went to study in Japan and got a job with a Japanese company in Jakarta right after graduation; then he bought a Japanese car, then got a mortgage, then met the right girl through a friend of a friend. This girl, he found out pretty quickly, was not a virgin and had had her heart broken to pieces by some guy, but she had little ambition and was therefore suitable to be his partner, and later, would probably be a less demanding housewife and mother. They wed, but, like Dara's previous boyfriend, this man isn't very interested in her. Thus, he will listen to Dara's answer to his question, but his attention will be on the dead television screen, the tablecloth, the carpet under their feet (*there are biscuit crumbs*, he thinks), as well as on their Muji cutlery, and on a sliver of bright light from the balcony of a neighbouring apartment. He wears glasses that he cleans compulsively with the hem of his shirt/T-shirt/pyjama top every few minutes. Dara always says, 'I went for a walk.' 'I watched the news broadcast on the NHK channel.' 'I'm studying Japanese so I can make friends.' Now they have been married for two, three years. At the beginning of the year they moved to Osaka, because her husband got a job at the Osaka branch of the company where he works, transferring from the Jakarta branch. The fact is that Dara doesn't have friends. That night Dara slowly spoons her food; it is a bowl of clear soup, which she pours half-heartedly back into the bowl. *She* always sits with her back to the kitchen. Instead of answering, *I went for a walk*, as usual, for some reason this time Dara chooses to say, 'I saw that Japanese woman again.'

Her husband lets out a bored yawn; sleepy tears well up in his eyes. 'What woman?' he says.

You always studied everything carefully. Before you finally decided to take pills, you first conducted research on the various ways you could choose to 'do it', along with their levels of pain and inconvenience. It is surprising that there are so many options for somebody who wants to die. You read dozens of suicide stories on the internet and sought inspiration from films and books. One day, while sitting in the corner of a remote cafe in Umeda, Osaka, where nobody cared about you, you classified the methods and listed them in your little notebook as follows:

> Slashing open a vein — on the wrist, arm, or neck
> Drowning — in the bathtub, oceans, lakes
> Jumping — from a tall building (Tsutenkaku Tower?),
>   from apartment balcony
> Ingesting — insecticide, sleeping pills, cleaning agents
> Throwing oneself in front of a train, or freeway traffic
> Other means, including — guns, stop eating/drinking,
>   hanging

Your order arrived — a plate of cheesecake with strawberry sauce — but you paid without even touching it and went straight to your apartment to continue your research. You surfed the internet until two in the morning. When you fell asleep, you dreamed of committing suicide. When you woke up, you thought about having a small breakfast of cereal, then concluded that: slashing open a vein is too painful, drowning is too scary, jumping is too messy and will traumatise other people, and so is throwing oneself into some form of public transportation (what if people just want to go to work but they see your body strewn across the platform of the Namba underground station?); you didn't know how to obtain a gun, starving oneself is tiring and time consuming, and hanging had a greater chance of failure, and if you succeeded it would likely make you suffer longer than necessary. So, you chose to ingest something that would end your life. Your choice fell on those sleeping pills.

These days Dara and her husband are trying to conceive, and have been failing for months, when Dara finds out who the Japanese woman is, what *kind* of woman she is. One night, just as the app on her mobile reminded Dara that her fertile window had opened again, she and her husband were lying side by side on the bed, under a dim light, when her husband said, 'Hey, maybe we should try something new, so we don't get bored.' And Dara then saw her, on the screen of her husband's new laptop. She appeared without warning, like a miracle. Her husband did not say anything else; he was busy choosing videos from a porn site without worrying at all about how Dara might be feeling. Apparently, the woman had a pair of pointy breasts whose areolas were pale white but whose nipples were pink. Her breasts were supple, not small, but not very large, and therefore they must have been real. It was an old video, according to the year on the screen. Apparently, her genitals were cleanly shaven. Apparently, she could groan, could sweat, could speak. *Kimochi*, she said. That was all her dialogue, repeated over and over again between sighs and moans. Even with her minimal Japanese proficiency, Dara knew what the word meant: *so nice*. Apparently, she could have sex with two, three men at once. *Was it good?* thought Dara. Suddenly, she remembered seeing the same woman on the screen of her husband's mobile when he had fallen asleep in the middle of scrolling Instagram. But at that time Dara hadn't thought about anything; she hadn't cared, she just took her husband's mobile from between their pillows and returned it to the nightstand. She hadn't paid any attention to what account her husband had been looking at. Now her husband was no longer lying down because he was busy with his laptop, which had been moved to their bed and onto his lap from the table; he was completely absorbed with the porn site. Dara sat up, hesitated.

'Fun, right?' said her husband. He glanced at Dara, then turned back to the screen. What should she, Dara, say? Apparently, the Japanese woman is her, Dara wanted to say, her index finger wanted to point. But she said nothing. Now what should she do?

'So we don't get bored,' her husband said again.

Are you bored? Dara thought, even though the answer was obvious.

Her husband moved the laptop back onto the table but left the video of the woman playing in the background. One of his hands was cupping one of Dara's breasts. The remaining one reached under her. Her husband was big and strong, even though he looked like an innocent young boy, and his hands were strong and wide like an iron shovel. They made love — if there was any love involved. Dara reminded herself to lie still for ten to fifteen minutes after her husband ejaculated inside her, both legs lifted in the air, a pillow tucked under her pelvis. It wasn't nice, wasn't kimochi. 'Nice' is a word to describe rice balls. The video was almost fifteen minutes long, so for a few minutes after her husband's ejaculation, Dara fixed her gaze on the woman, who was staring back at her from the screen. Is she alright? Can she breathe under such pressure? Suddenly Dara wanted to cry, her chest felt tight. Occasionally she does allow herself to cry at these times, because she knows her husband won't notice.

Onscreen, a man ejaculated in the woman's body. To Dara, that man was faceless; her mind was full only of the woman's face.

It was a Thursday afternoon, and your heart decided to go to a pharmacy.

Your body had no choice but to comply. Your mind, on the other hand, had gone through various studies in cyberspace on ways of committing suicide to avoid mistakes or failure. You'd taken notes. You already knew that in Japan, the sleeping pills consumed by people with insomnia are benzodiazepines — such as zolpidem (Myslee), eszopiclone (Lunesta), ramelteon (Rozerem), or lorazepam, flurazepam, and estazolam — and these drugs cannot be obtained without a doctor's prescription. You couldn't go to see a doctor because you didn't suffer from physical, physiological, psychological, psychiatric, or pharmacological insomnia (unfortunately, you fell asleep easily and then had sweet dreams, which distressed you afterwards because reality was never as beautiful). Therefore, your choice was narrowed to sleeping pills that could be bought over the counter. (So you wouldn't cheat anyone, harm anyone.) You knew the safe dosage so that you could be sure to take an unsafe dose.

The brands you had listed were: Drewell, Neoday, Mylest S, Gu-Slee P, Oyasumi-na, and Restamin. All of them contain the same active ingredients — namely the first-generation antihistamine diphenhydramine — but because you liked the practicality, you had chosen Daiichi Sankyo's Gu-Slee P, one tablet of which already contained 50 milligrams of diphenhydramine. The maximum dose is only 50 milligrams per day. You bought four boxes of Gu-Slee P, each containing six tablets, that cost you 7600 yen. The man at the counter gave you all you asked for, noting that the sleeping pills would cause an anticholinergic reaction due to the diphenhydramine in them, which could mean mild side effects, such as a dry mouth, the morning after. 'It's okay,' you said, 'I know.' He suddenly looked surprised and said, 'Aren't you Yamazaki Chika?' But you shook your head. 'I don't know her,' you said sweetly. Then the man looked embarrassed; you watched the blush appear on his cheeks as if you had just slapped him.

You walked away. You repeated the trip to different pharmacies for a week until you had plenty. On one occasion, you looked at Drewell's packaging and wondered why it contained an image of a cute cat. Your mind told you, recalling an article on the internet, that Drewell was an abbreviation of 'dream well'. Well, your heart didn't want sweet dreams, and your body needed a long, endless deep sleep. So you had made the right choice. Good night. Goodbye.

———

As usual, Dara has written down these words on a piece of paper: *ninshin kensayaku, kudasai* and another piece of paper with the kanji characters 妊娠検査薬, which she had carefully copied from the internet a few months ago with a trembling hand, to be reused again and again. To Dara, the kanji characters will always look like overlapping pieces of grass, no matter how long she has been living in Japan, or how many years she has been married to her husband, who is fluent in reading, writing, and speaking Japanese. She has spent three whole minutes standing behind the kitchen counter, staring at the scraps of paper with the words and the kanji. In her head, without her wanting it, the words 'sumimasen nihongo wakarimasen' keep repeating. *Sorry, I don't understand Japanese.* Dara goes to the pharmacy.

This one is a different pharmacy from the one she used to visit, which is the only one nearby: just down the road, next to a shop that sells hiking gear and mountain bikes. This time she takes the bus a few blocks, even though there is a risk that she might get lost. Maybe she feels embarrassed, maybe she just doesn't want the friendly old woman, the pharmacist near her apartment, to find out that, for the umpteenth time, she is going to buy a pregnancy test, in between her regular schedule of buying aspirin for menstrual pain, as well as vitamin D. Maybe she doesn't want the old woman to think, *Stupid girl, why not buy a few packs at once so you don't have to go back and forth every month?* Or, *Why isn't that girl pregnant yet? What a pity.* The pharmacist behind the counter at this other one, far away, is a middle-aged man who is not as friendly as the old woman. He doesn't smile. Since he is a man, he won't even know what it is like. He won't think, *Oh poor girl.*

As usual Dara finds herself forgetting what she had wanted to say. 'Eh. Um.'

The place is very bright and clinical. She is desperate to glance at the scraps of paper in her pocket, when she suddenly sees the boxes of pregnancy-test kits sitting on the shelf near the pharmacist. She has used one or two of these specific brands several times and can easily recognise the packaging. Dara points. The middle-aged man behind the counter immediately understands, but his eyes are saying, *Stupid tourist*. Or maybe Dara is imagining it? She doesn't know. When she arrives home, she lets the pieces of paper remain in her pocket. She boils water and makes tea.

She will have to wait until tomorrow morning for the test kits to be effective. Now she will get groceries for dinner. This afternoon, she scribbles a shopping note: *mushrooms, onions, baking paper, two cartons of full-fat fresh milk, spinach, eggs, artichoke hearts*. She goes grocery shopping for the three hundred and twelfth time.

These days the Japanese woman will sometimes be seen sitting alone in a park, or standing for a few minutes at a crossroad, waiting for the traffic lights to turn green so she can cross — she waits patiently even though there are no cars passing by. One time Dara was right behind her, then next to her; her heart was pounding. Dara only needed to take two, three steps to get closer to the woman. The traffic light was still red, but there were no cars passing by, so Dara walked past her to cross. The woman waited for the green light with great patience, as if she really loved life. Who knows, there might suddenly be a car speeding through, right?

Dara didn't look back. Besides, her hands were full of groceries.

These days when her husband is at work, Dara barely talks to other human beings except for her mother, who calls her via WhatsApp at unexpected times. Dara, always patiently and without interrupting, listens to her chatter, her daily complaints, her gossip about every member of their large and problematic extended family. She always listens. Her mother occasionally asks about her, then inevitably, she'll ask if there are any signs that she has become pregnant. Dara will shake her head even though her mother won't be able to see it. She'll say out loud, 'No', then one way or another, her mother will say, 'What kind of women are we if we can't have kids?' After countless repetitions of this dynamic, Dara has become accustomed to the heartache. After each conversation, she simply goes to sleep to relieve her headache. She is a good daughter, so good that, in her entire life, she has only defended herself once in front of her mother, when she blamed Dara after her ex-boyfriend broke off their engagement. 'It's not Dara's fault, Ma,' she had screamed. In all her life, only once did she ever get out of control and cry in front of her mother, who hasn't actually been a very good one, come to think of it.

Then it was a Friday morning, and you were not really doing anything because you had marked that Friday as the day of your death.

Your body was gliding from room to room.

Your body stopped moving, and your mind commanded it to close the curtains. Then you remembered that you had to make sure that all electronic devices were turned off and that there were no taps on in the house.

You once hung twelve origami cranes from the ceiling, which would be called *senbazuru* if there were a thousand of them. If you have a thousand, then you can make a wish. You tried to remember what kind of wish you were trying to make when you had gone to a Kinokuniya in Namba a long time ago, bought ten packs of washi paper, brought them home, and started folding the cranes one by one to be hung from the ceiling when you had made a thousand. You tried to remember why you had given up after the twelfth crane.

You pictured the washi papers back then, scattered on the table in so many colours and patterns. Back then, you had started with one that was honey yellow in colour and had a pattern of *hanashobu* flowers. To fold an origami crane, you start by folding the paper in four diagonally, and then repeating it on the opposite side vertically. Follow the twelve-step instructions and finish by blowing air into the crane's abdominal cavity. Repeat a thousand times. Make your wish.

At your apartment, you had finished making sure that all the electronics and taps were turned off. The electronic devices included your mobile phone, and that meant no one could reach you from that moment on. Then you climbed up on the dressing chair to remove the cranes from the ceiling. They fell gracefully onto the carpet, as if someone had broken their paper wings. You watched them pile up from the height of the dressing chair. Your carpet was grey, and the birds were colourful — blue, pink, light-green, and purple. The threads that held them together were strewn across the carpet like hairs or veins. You got off the chair. For a moment you thought, maybe the person who would find that chair there would think you were going to hang yourself? Then you returned the chair to its original place near the dressing table.

You took your sweet time counting each minute that passed by just because you wanted to kill time a bit more than killing yourself.

What does she want to say to the woman? 'Um, last night my husband masturbated while watching your video again. He sat on his chair, so his sperm spurted onto the desk, and then he took some tissues to wipe it off, cleaning it all up, afterwards. He didn't touch me, he seemed to forget that I was in the room. Um, what does it feel like to be you? What are you like, what is your life like? I just want to know.' Maybe Dara would chatter frantically, her sentences gushing out of her mouth uncontrollably like vomit. But *sumimasen nihongo wakarimasen*.

Autumn. Dara sees that the Japanese woman is looking up at the shedding trees. In autumn, we will be expecting *momiji*, that's what people here call it; its meaning is when the leaves change their colours to various shades of red, orange, and yellow — all is pure beauty and splendour. But in fact, we will often be disappointed to find that in the middle of the city, most of the leaves are simply dying or stubbornly staying green, creeping up concrete walls. To witness momiji, one has to visit some other prettier, more remote places. Kyoto and Nara are only an hour by train from Osaka; to Kobe, it is less than an hour. One can go there. Osaka, meanwhile, is just another big city. There are only concrete buildings, grey sidewalks, the LUCUA 1100 shopping centre devouring half of Umeda Station like a giant monster in Japanese comic books, as well as the spacious BIC Camera store that beams so brash and bright it almost seems insolent. There are only millions of megawatts of multicoloured neon lights blinding our eyes, especially throughout Dōtonbori (the famous street-food haven), where lonely souls remain lonely despite being caught up in a crowd, so crowded that these lonely bodies crash into each other. Dara imagines the woman's body in the same kind of setting: it swims bravely through the vapour from the food stalls, amongst thousands of people, and then stops to buy steaming-hot *okonomiyaki* fresh from the hot plate. The food seller will probably be the only human who exchanges pleasantries with the woman's body after an entire day. Then the woman's body will find a plastic stool by the side of the road. Then a strange man may approach and ask her, *Want to eat with me?*

They are as lonely as we are.

She, the Japanese woman, looks up at the shedding trees, but not for long. A moment later she starts to walk away. Her steps are a little shuffled, like she's exhausted, but she is still beautiful, a shining angel. It's annoying and unfair. For a moment, Dara looks at the same trees the woman was looking at. *You know, it's not the trees' fault that their leaves turn an ugly dry brown and fall to the ground and onto the sidewalk, instead of becoming a pretty blushing thing like you are.* Now she knows what she wants to say:

'This morning, I went to the toilet after my husband had left. He always leaves the house very early in the morning, he says to avoid the crowds of people on the train on their way to work. I had been there too, in that crowd, although on purpose. At seven, eight in the morning, I once went to Umeda Station, and stood there in the middle of all those people who had actual things to do with their lives. I was immediately immersed in a sea of white shirts and black suits, heads full of black hair, swirls of neat skirts. I watched them. Their faces were obedient and unhappy. They were like me. But they walked swiftly and quickly, because they knew where they were going. To be there means to be swept away in the fast currents of a fierce river. Nobody saw me, I saw them. My husband might have still been among them, I don't know. I didn't see my husband. Neither did I see you.

'So this morning I went to the toilet. The first day we moved into this apartment, I was shocked to discover how small the toilet was. I hated being there and was afraid to be there, but then I felt at home, because in there, it felt like being held close and being loved. Gradually I have grown to enjoy lingering with myself in a room so small, a room that hugs me so tightly that I forget to open all the social media apps on my phone. I used to torture myself like that. I depended on my phone to keep up with people at home without having to ask, as well as to be made envious by the happiness of others, by photos of laughter and parties, pictures of babies, pictures of small children sticking out little fat hands in the air so that their mother would pick them up and hug them. Then, gradually, my phone began to function only as a timer while I spent time with myself in the toilet. Poor toilet. Every month, there are certain times when the narrow space of this toilet has to accommodate the breadth of my fears, my yearning, and my sadness. Every time I finish peeing on each of the 妊娠検査薬 plastic sticks. As usual *ninshin kensayaku, kudasai*. This morning too, as usual, I didn't find a plus sign or two red lines: only a minus sign, and one red line on the cheapest and least sophisticated plastic stick. Try again next month? This morning I sat for a long time in my toilet and thought that I was tired and wanted to sleep for a long time and never wake up again.

'Do you want to know? The first time I did it, it came out positive, but then I lost it, my baby.'

The Japanese woman's body glides from one intersection to another. Dara walks faster — she doesn't want to lose her.

———

Rainy season. On those days Dara always wanted the kind of snack they say every woman would want early in their pregnancy: all things fresh and sour, pickles and unripe mangoes. Even so, she was really alright, she wasn't nauseous or bothered by all kinds of smells, and her tongue did not need to always be comforted by sour things. But now she just wanted it. Period. After work, she visited the Ranch Market closest to her office in the Mega Kuningan Circle to get some ridiculous rujak guava for a ridiculously high price. Two weeks earlier she'd unexpectedly had positive pregnancy test results. That afternoon she smiled at the plastic rujak guava box and at the cashier who asked if she wanted a plastic bag for her shopping. Rain. She did want a plastic bag, thank you very much. She imagined that the plastic box would be safe from the rain because it was protected by a plastic bag, just as the alien being would be — the being that she had not known for very long yet — safe from the rain because it was protected by the amniotic fluid, organs, and layers of fibres in Dara's body; including her tunic, a little wrinkled after a long day of work. So the extraterrestrial swam around in Dara's body while she swam in the rain. She scampered across the puddly road to get into a taxi, whose driver kept grumbling along the way, complaining about everything from traffic jams to Jokowi. But it didn't matter. That evening at seven o'clock, she had her first pregnancy check-up scheduled at the mother-and-child hospital in central Jakarta. Her husband was off to Japan for work. It was okay, really. It was a rainy Friday evening.

She remembered asking the extraterrestrial, through the power of her mind, what it wanted to do for the weekend. The two of them could go somewhere, just the two of them; watch a movie or have a nice meal. Its body was still so small, as small as nothing, and it would answer her in the language of extraterrestrials, its sentences the bile that was flowing out of Dara's liver, its words a compound of salt, cholesterol, and bilirubin. *What do you want to eat tonight? Do you have a soul?*

She had read: according to Aristotle, a foetus has a soul at the age of 40 days for boys and 90 days for girls. According to the Catholic church, the foetus has been human since fertilisation. Medically, this can be determined based on a variety of different factors. By law, it's determined according to when the foetus can survive outside the womb, and there are various sub-things under it. None of it is sensible, but isn't this baby-nothing just adorable nonetheless?

You had read: *side effects include dry mouth and others depending on the dosage of use.* You looked at the packaging of the sleeping pills. You sat on your bed, leaning on two pillows. You had put on a lacy satin nightgown. You had also prepared a bottle of water, because one glass would definitely not be enough.

Rain. She still remembers feeling annoyed that her ob-gyn was dry and comfortable in her chair, while Dara'd had to jog a little bit through the rain after getting out of the taxi. She had been shivering while waiting for her turn in the fancy but tired hospital corridor. During the consultation, the ob-gyn stared at the rainwater that seemed about to stream from the tips of Dara's hair, but didn't, as if it were hesitating. She remembers that the doctor was a young woman, like she herself was. She did not ask, *Where is your husband?* Dara remembers thinking, aimlessly, that she didn't mind whether the ob-gyn was a man or a woman, but it seemed strange to let an unfamiliar man reach into our genitals while we lay on a long, sterile, unimaginably wide sheet of tissue paper, stretching down the cold patient bed; our legs wide apart. 'My hands are a bit cold, forgive me, Ma'am,' said the doctor after washing her hands in the sink; she sincerely apologised. Dara's doctor — her name was Melani, if she's not mistaken — rubbed her hands together then pressed them against her own cheeks to warm them. 'My husband is abroad,' Dara told her, even though no one had asked.

She remembers, despite the precautionary measures, how cold Dr Melani's hands were on various places on Dara's body, how cold the lubricating gel was that she slathered on the condom that covered the tip of the endovaginal ultrasound wand. The thing penetrated Dara's genitals. It felt like a penis, with that ridiculous condom and all, but it pierced deeper. She grimaced a little. She remembers lying down, staring at the screen above their heads and wondering why it was so high up.

She remembers seeing nothing.

'There's nothing here,' mumbled Dr Melani, seemingly more to herself. Then to Dara, she said softly, 'There is only a sac, the foetus hasn't developed.'

She remembers not crying when she called her husband in Japan to deliver the news. Blighted ovum, that's the term. Empty. She told her husband about the schedule for vacuum aspiration at the hospital so that Dara's body could be cleansed of the remains of the extraterrestrial, if there were indeed any, and the details were such: five, six weeks until everything is normal again, there may be heavy bleeding, maybe not, they will check again later; no exercise, no heavy lifting, no sexual intercourse. She remembers asking if her husband could return to Jakarta to accompany her during the procedure. She remembers, after the procedure, standing for a long time in the bathroom, rolling up bloody pads and each time looking to see if there was a body, so small that it was barely there. But there was nothing.

She will never forget what it was like to lie under the bright light, legs spread wide, coughing once, twice, because the doctor told her to cough (what if she refused? What could they do then?); the bright light of the lamp, an immense sheet of sterile tissue paper under her body; her body wrapped in a hospital gown over her own clothes (she chose a loose skirt because she thought she'd want to be able to move freely afterward); a clean smell, the injection of a local anaesthetic that was like the bite of a very small ant somewhere in her vagina but she didn't know where exactly, so deep inside it; her husband waited outside, saying nothing; an iron tool opened access to her birth canal, she remembers that the chill was rather faint; she remembers a tool or a long tube sticking in, a clean smell, a small screen somewhere nearby to guide the doctor's work, and Dara didn't want to see it; she remembers a strange deep pain, a caress on her arm, a calming nurse talking softly to her and constantly, slowly stroking her; the nurse's eyes were saying, *Poor girl*; a hum of the engine, the indecent sound of the engine sucking, slurping inside her; she always remembers the faint pain and then her eyes burned and then her tears pooled. Then, *Clean*, someone said.

She remembers the clean smell, the soothing words of everyone.

She can never forget.

Meanwhile, one by one, the sleeping pills started to enter your body. Your heart refused to pause, refused to stop, because you were afraid that doubts would creep in. A famous musician once sang these lyrics, didn't he? There are cracks, cracks in everything, that's how light can enter. Your heart didn't want any light to enter your body; only the pills could enter.

You were not crying. In fact, your stomach was full of water and sleeping pills and your mind was focused on the bloating sensation. Your body was now lying on its back, staring at the ceiling. Your phone was lying on the side table and its Pikachu charm was looking at you questioningly.

She is such a tiny insignificant human. We are familiar with that sensation — being small amidst countless other humans at an intersection when the traffic lights turn green and the crowd rushes across like a flood. We always see this kind of scene in movies, shot from above to underline the reality of how small we are in this universe, how anonymous. The view is of a large city in Japan, usually Tokyo, that famous intersection in Shibuya. Did you know that the Shibuya Crossing is the busiest intersection in the world? Now, this isn't Tokyo, but Osaka isn't that different. People won't know the difference, Tokyo or Osaka. From above, people would not be able to pinpoint where Dara is and where the Japanese woman is. Dara is as small as a grain of fragrant Japanese rice. She is rolling around everywhere. The woman trots and scuttles through. Dara runs after her.

What am I going to do, what do I want to do? Dara wants to touch the woman, feel her skin, count her moles one by one, those that she had seen in her adult videos on the glowing screen. There were three of them on the woman's back: they were a constellation of stars in another galaxy. She wants to say: 'My husband has fallen in love with you or has always loved you. It's okay, I don't love him either — I just want to know why I don't deserve to be happy, and maybe you can explain it to me. Why I can't have children. Do you have children? What kind of girl are you? Autumn. Not only do the leaves and tree branches dry up, but my skin and lips do as well, the skin of my lips would harden in the dry cold wind, then split open. If I smile, I'll bleed. You never smile at the convenience store cashier, and you never buy anything, and thus you don't bleed. But I've seen you bleed. *That* video is archived under the category of "virgin/Asian/teen". You let a strange, blue-haired man fuck you until you bled, the camera aiming from below, like an excited little dog who likes to sniff at people's groins. Did it hurt? I just want to know. I saw your blood dripping, soaking onto the white sheet, mixed with the white foam of the semen belonging to the blue-haired man. My husband said he married a girl who was no longer a virgin (it was me), but who cares, nowadays no girl is still a virgin anyway. Do you know? My name, Dara, means virgin girl. This is my secret joke.

'I also want to tell you, this morning I didn't cry in the toilet at those negative test results. Instead, I sat peeling the dry skin off my lips because it felt good, and the sting was unbearable. The blood dripped into my mouth and spread across my tongue, and I drank it. Do you know? The blood from the cracks on our lips is actually very difficult to stop. The blood will seep out for hours, little by little, and our mouths will smell of iron all day long. If you apply lip balm, the balm stick will be stained with red. If we smile, we will bleed even more, then the blood will mix with the components of fat and aloe vera of the lip balm, and it won't dry out because it can't dry out. What the hell am I talking about? I don't know. People will look at us because of our lips that are damaged here and there, and they will think, *why doesn't that girl hide her hideous lips with a really dark or really red lipstick*? That's what will happen: after we have finished painstakingly peeling off all the dry bits, our lips will be discoloured, some parts looking normal and some parts looking like raw meat. People will flinch, they can't help but feel the pain, and they will silently scold us because of it.'

I am now following you, but then people's faces slowly drip off their heads. I stand here, stunned, for a moment. I steal a glance at the puddle of faces on the sidewalk, secretly, because I'm afraid people will get angry if they notice that I'm staring at their faces as they fall to the ground. I don't know what's going on. They just keep on rushing, footsteps splashing through a pair of cheeks full of pimples or cheeks smeared with Shiseido blush, feet stepping on pairs of eyes gazing up at the sky, heels penetrating breathing nostrils and silent lips; the faces melt and melt. A faceless young man, in the Japanese 'sailor' high-school uniform with a scarf draped around his neck, passes by me while looking at a phone with a brightly lit screen, but how can he see? His eyes have become a puddle on the pavement. Is he chatting with a loved one or cheating on a loved one? Without lips, how will he be able to convey his feelings? Then I become terrified because, if you are now also faceless, I won't know how to recognise you. However, you are still several metres ahead of me. I know very well the details of your face because I look at you so often. Wide eyes. A pair of eyebrows arched slightly upward. We veer onto a smaller road, leaving the crowded area, where people's faces on the sidewalk might cause us to slip. It is Friday night, seven o'clock. Every corner of the city of Osaka is filled with light. Young people fill up ramen stalls and roadside bars, stepping in pairs in the middle of the bustle of shopping centres. The old ones fill up the *go* play area, staring at the black-and-white stones on the game board. Lonely men and women are sitting in front of convenience stores, smoking, relaxed, not thinking of having to catch a train, not worrying about having to go home because no one is waiting for them at home. Tourists walk briskly on the sidewalks, even though they're exhausted after a full day touring the city. Young mothers pass by on bicycles, their children safely seated behind them. Slowly and unhurriedly, their faces drip off their heads, sliding down the streets, splattering everywhere.

You remain calm, striding steadily towards your destination. You are going home.

I should have realized that you are a ghost. That Friday, the first day of November, a semi-famous Japanese adult-film star had decided to end her life by swallowing several dozen sleeping pills in her apartment in the Umeda area of Osaka. Yamazaki Chika, whose real name was Onda Ayaka, died at the age of thirty. The motive of her suicide is unknown, but police have concluded that there are no signs of foul play. Originally from Yokohama, she was living alone, and her body was not found until Sunday afternoon by her manager, who became worried that nobody had been able to contact the star for nearly three days. The manager was faceless. He went trotting into the apartment building of his client, his rubber-soled shoes squeaking along the empty corridor. He stood there, pressing Onda Ayaka's doorbell for a full five minutes. 'Are you in there?' he shrieked (but how, since he had no lips?). 'Are you in there?' Then he began to notice the fleeting, faint rotten stench, unfathomable but real, seeping through the gap under the door and, suddenly panicking, he shouted, 'Hey, you in there?!' (How did he smell it, with no nose?) He freaked out and called building management until a faceless person arrived with a duplicate key. What he saw behind the door made the manager drop his phone on the floor while screaming (but without eyes, how could he see you?). Nothing felt real. (You would have said, 'I've only been sleeping for two days, I need to sleep more.')

But even after all that, people would still recognise you as the beautiful Yamazaki Chika, the semi-famous adult-film star. The difference was that you were now only a body. Time of death: approximately two days prior. Cause of death: suicide, overdose of sleeping pills. Your body had passed through the algor mortis stage and had entered the rigor mortis stage; your skin had turned grey-green, and fluid was starting to fill the cavities. Now your body lived on its own because the body is a body, an organism in itself; to be declared dead, your soul is what has to die. And that Sunday, when they found you, the bacteria in your intestines had replaced your soul to continue living; they had reproduced and were eating your beautiful body from within.

A few days later, people would learn about the tragedy in the newspapers.

Because I don't know that, though, I keep chasing you. Somewhere in the distance, there has been a pandemic that makes people's faces melt and fall onto the pavement. You will show me a safe place, you will be the only person whom I can identify. I'll be safe with you.

I am now in an apartment in the Umeda area of Osaka. The corridors are narrow but very bright: bright from white neon lamps. You're wearing low heels that don't make any sound on the floor that would have echoed along these narrow but very bright corridors. Then suddenly you turn to me. '*Sumimasen nihongo wakarimasen*,' I mutter. 'I'm really sorry, I don't understand Japanese, Ayaka.' But you understand. 'Come in, come on in.' You say you want to be friends. You open the door and I walk in behind you.

I am in an apartment. It is pitch black, except for a ray of moonlight that pierces through the gap in the curtain. Behind the curtain, there is a sliding glass door, behind the sliding glass door is a balcony. Light always enters through cracks and gaps, Ayaka. But thanks to the light, I can see where I'm going without hitting the sharp corners of furniture. A dead television screen. Tablecloth. A rug under the dining table and chairs (biscuit crumbs on the carpet, I see). Muji cutlery. Beams of bright light from the balcony of the neighbouring apartment.

You lead me to a room. What do you want to show me? I don't know yet, but three days after your death, your manager had come and pounded on your door, and he would find what you now want to show me. You open the door.

There, on the bed, the body of a woman lies facing the ceiling of the room. She is wearing a lacy satin nightgown, and her head is supported by two stacked pillows. There is a plastic bottle on the nightstand, containing a puddle of water, not a puddle of face; it is just an ordinary bottle of Minami mineral water. You are telling me, *That girl has gone to sleep.*

That girl is me.

My hesitation is brief. I approach myself and sit on the bed beside that body. I stroke her face; I remove a few strands of hair that are scattered on her cheeks. 'You are so beautiful,' I tell her. 'Like an angel.'

Elegy:
These days there is a strange kind of peace wrapping around them both. As the man makes coffee, a mechanical rumbling from the coffee machine fills the apartment, almost like the sound of a sore stomach, but familiar to the ears, a

153

sound reminiscent of home and morning. Since the man is making breakfast, there is the buzzing sound of a microwave for two, and then three minutes, with a bowl of oatmeal rotating in place, bathing in yellow light until the microwave finally gives a loud chime, the sign that the five minutes are over. Then three more minutes, because the man has to heat up another bowl. Since the man wants to watch NHK, the television is on, providing the mumble of a human voice speaking in the background. The voice is speaking Japanese and the man understands every word, even though he is not Japanese. Because his phone rings occasionally, he will talk (if he doesn't have to talk, he prefers silence; it feels peaceful). 'I slept enough, but now I'm awake, really,' he says softly, not wanting to spoil the silence around him. 'We're just having breakfast.' It's half past eight in the morning. The man tilts his head, tucks his mobile phone against his left shoulder as he places two bowls of oatmeal on the dining table. His wife sits in her usual chair, fixing her gaze on the top of the Umeda Sky that is visible from the window. 'Dara, please stop, yeah?' says the man, because his wife is again peeling off the dry skin on her lips. She is busy with a wide layer of the driest skin, two fingers prying and tugging, leaving a bloody trail that looks very painful. 'Come on, let's eat. Come.' The man smiles. His wife stops peeling her lips. When his wife smiles, a drop of blood pools on her lower lip, seeping out of a crack there. The man takes a deep breath to calm himself, then he says to his mother on the phone, 'We're coming home next week, Ma. All is well; Dara is better.' Of course his mother is worried. All of them in Jakarta are worried, but things are getting better. His wife scoops out the oatmeal, studying him. What is she thinking? Who knows? His mother-in-law had also asked, crying, what her daughter was thinking, but who knows. *She is lonely here*, the man had said. *And we lost a child*. For some reason, he and his wife never told anyone about it. Maybe because it doesn't feel real? Maybe because they were afraid people would say, *what child?* After all, the child never existed, it disappeared before it really existed. 'Dara is sad, Ma,' said the man, 'we are having trouble conceiving. Yes, see you at the airport. You also take care of yourself.' He disconnects the WhatsApp call. His wife, meanwhile, has finished her portion. 'Coffee?' asks the man, and his wife nods. Maybe it never happened, and his wife never overdosed on paracetamol; the paramedic never pumped her stomach in the local hospital's emergency room; the man never sat waiting in the corridor with his guts churning. But now, on television, Takase Kozo switches to reading the news about the death of Onda Ayaka, the semi-famous adult-film actor. They are still reporting it after some time. The man swallows hard. '*That* one is real,' he muses, as if his wife's action hadn't been real. He feels miserable again but reminds himself that things have improved. He turns off the television.

He turns around to pour the coffee. In her chair, his wife is still looking at the top of the Umeda Sky building in the distance. One hand floats back to her face, her index finger and thumb working slowly and carefully. But now she doesn't just peel off the dry skin on her lips — she peels off her lips, entirely, until there is nothing left. Her lips fall onto the table.

ACKNOWLEDGEMENTS

I would first like to thank Norman Erikson Pasaribu and Leopold Adisurya Indrawan, the first readers of this book. Without their valuable advice and support, it could not have been written.

Birth Canal has also been supported by: The Jakarta Arts Council Writing Academy; Asialink, The University of Melbourne; Australian Indonesian Institute; and Salihara Arts Community, who kindly granted and funded the 'Tulis' writing residency in Australia.

An extract from 'Rukmini' was published by InterSastra, made possible by the invitation of Eliza Vitri Handayani and the hard work of Julia Winterflood.

For the publication of the Indonesian edition, I would like to thank Kepustakaan Populer Gramedia and, in particular, my editors: Christina Udiani, an incredible help and a source of inspiration, and Udji Kayang.

The English edition wouldn't have happened without Laura Elizabeth Woollett, Marika Webb-Pullman, and Scribe Publications.

I owe many aspects of my career to Nirwan Dewanto and Ayu Utami, and finally, I owe everything to my husband, Renke Pieter Meuwese, whose insights and assistance contributed immensely to the English translation.